RED FEVER

CAROLINE CLOUGH

CLASS:	JF:CLO	
NUMBER:	J13427F1848	
	2014	£5.99	BRAINS

 Kelpies

Kelpies is an imprint of Floris Books

First published in 2010 by Floris Books
Third printing 2014
© 2010 Caroline Clough

The publisher acknowledges subsidy from
Creative Scotland towards the publication of this
volume.

 This book is also available
as an eBook

MIX
Paper from
responsible sources
FSC **FSC® C023114**
www.fsc.org

British Library CIP data available
ISBN 978-086315-776-9
Printed in Great Britain
by Page Bros Ltd.

To all my family

1. A Mad Mission

A heavy white mist clung to the world, blurring the edges between sea and sky. Toby crouched low on the front deck of the boat as it sliced slowly through the grey waters. His eyes strained through the murkiness, alert to any danger that may lie ahead. The damp air seeped through his clothes and he shivered with cold but also with fear of what he had to do next. This was a mission Toby might not return from. His dad was mad to even think of it.

"Dad! Whoa! Slow down," Toby cried. "I think I can see something. About twenty metres ahead."

"Keep watch for any rubbish!" his dad shouted from the wheelhouse, as he steered round the floating flotsam of plastic drums, bottles and a scum of random litter.

The purr of the boat's engine fell to a stutter and the boat rolled lazily on the oily swell. As Toby hung as far out as he dared from the bow and peered through the fog, a slight breeze lifted and cleared the path ahead.

"Dad! Look!" Toby gasped. Looming through the whiteness, towering over the boat, the large rusted legs of the oil platform came into view. Toby fell backwards as his eyes followed the height of the legs from sea level up and up until they disappeared into the grey gloom.

"Toby! Get ready!" his dad commanded.

Toby picked himself up and grabbed the rope with shaking hands. He could now hear the ghostly creaking of the giant structure as it sighed and groaned in the surging sea, and he could see the twisted red-brown girders hanging high above his head as the boat bobbed underneath. So this was what an oil platform looked like after it had been left to the ravages of the sea for three years. His dad had worked on one similar to this, but further out into the North Sea.

"Are you ready, Toby?" his dad barked.

"Yep!" Toby replied, leaning out from the bow, the thick heavy rope coiled in his hands, ready to throw it on to anything it would catch on. Some of the diagonal bracing struts had been smashed by storms and dangled uselessly in mangled knots of metal from above. With a grunt Toby threw the looped end of the rope over a broken spar.

Strange to think that he, Toby Tennant, had never even been on such a boat until a year ago. He'd hated sailing. Now, here he was expertly tying one up to an oil platform. Crazy.

"OK, Toby, get going."

"Yes, Dad."

"And be quick. There could be pirates in the area!"

Thanks, Dad! That's all I need — something else to worry about. As if this thing exploding or sinking whilst I'm on it isn't enough, thought Toby.

He climbed on to the side of the boat, and readied himself for the leap on to the rusted ladder that swung from the leg of the platform.

"Got the walkie-talkie?" His dad yelled out his last instructions.

Toby sprang like a cat, but just as he leapt a wave hit the side of the boat, swinging it and him away from the platform. With an extra effort he threw himself towards the corroded metal ladder. He didn't want to land in the freezing, dirty water. He wouldn't last long.

"Ah!" Toby cried as the force of the jump carried him bang up against the slimy seaweed-draped tower, and he landed heavily on a rung of the ladder.

"Oh!" Red-hot pain seared a path from his hand to his brain as his right hand took the brunt of the landing, caught between the ladder and the tower. The tower's patchwork of seaweed hid a coating of razor-sharp barnacles, encrusted on to the metal. Toby's nylon gloves ripped easily as his hand raked across the jagged shells, tearing a large bloody gash across his knuckles.

A wave of nausea washed over him as, through the fog of pain, he heard his dad shouting something about the wind getting up and to be quick.

Quick, thought Toby. *Must be quick.* He gritted his teeth and, pushing through the pain, forced himself to place his foot on the next rung of the ladder. The thick soles of his boot slithered forwards then found a grip on the slippery metal. He heaved himself up, using his good hand. As he climbed, the strong pungent smell of seaweed filled his nostrils and the noisy calls of hundreds of seagulls wheeling and diving around him made him feel dizzy.

It took all of Toby's strength to hoist himself up the twenty metres, placing his feet carefully on each rung to test if it would take his weight. As he removed his foot each time, pieces of rust scraped off to float slowly downwards into the murky space below.

Mustn't look down. Keep focused on going up; that's what Dad always says.

Toby tried to remember the rules of climbing, which his dad had taught him out on the sea cliffs near their home. That all seemed a very long time ago now. That was before all this — before the red fever had killed his grandparents, his friends, almost everyone he had ever known, and most of the population — before the world had gone mad.

"One elephant, two elephants, three ..." Toby tried counting aloud to match the rhythm of his slow ascent. His hand throbbed but he kept going.

He could now see the huge underbelly of the platform appearing from the mist. Ropes and bundles of wires and pipes hung down like giant strands of hair. He felt sick, whether it was from the pain in his hand or the fear which gripped his stomach, he didn't know.

Stop being such a baby, he told himself. *Get on with it.*

At last he could see an opening above. The next step up was on to solid metal steps and then up on to the top deck. There were even more seagulls nesting on the upper scaffolding. They were huge beasts, squawking and screaming at each other, squabbling over bits of litter. A couple of them spotted Toby and, stretching out their huge white wings, dive-bombed him with open beaks.

"Get lost, you morons!" he shouted, batting out at them with his good hand.

Toby ran along a walkway towards what looked like the entrance doors to the main block. He tried not to look through the metal grid floor to down below, where the angry sea could be glimpsed through the swirling mist.

The doors to the block were swinging gently, half off their hinges, creaking eerily in the salty breeze. He bashed through them, kicking aside the mounds of plastic bottles, papers and soggy cardboard boxes that the wind had blown in.

"What a stink!" Toby cried out, covering his nose with his cagoule sleeve. The ripe stench of rotting matter hit him as he pushed his way along the corridor.

Toby was aware of his heart pumping fit to burst. He felt his nerves, raw and on edge. He didn't know what he was going to find. Dead bodies? Skeletons picked clean by the seagulls? He scanned each room quickly as he passed it, but the place was bare apart from litter.

Toby felt uneasy, as if someone was watching him. He wanted to run and run so fast that his legs would skip over the waves and carry him home, to his real home. He wanted to wake up in his bed tucked under the eaves in his parents' cottage and find that this had all been a bad dream: that his little sister was well again and that his mum was alive.

GET A GRIP! Look! Keep looking! It's got to be here somewhere.

His dad had told him where the muster points would be for an emergency, where he would find a diagram and the location of the medical bay. But as panic started to take hold of him, his dad's plan flew from

Toby's head. He just wanted to find the medical bay —
now. He tried to push through large double doors but
the damp sea air had warped them and they were stuck
shut. He took a jump at them and kicked out hard with
his boots.

BANG! The doors burst open with a noise that echoed
through the whole empty building. Toby stopped and
listened. Was he imagining things or could he hear
someone singing? Was this what happened to mariners in
the old days? They went mad hearing noises and thought
mermaids were singing to them?

"Keep moving!" he shouted out. This was madness.
This whole idea was crazy. How could his dad do this to
him? How desperate must his dad have to be to send his
only son on to a deserted oil platform?

But Toby knew the answer. They *were* desperate. If
they didn't find help for Sylvie soon, it could be too late.

The canteen was scattered with broken tables and chairs.
At the back of the large room Toby could see the kitchens.
Someone had broken all the plates and cups and saucers.
The floor was covered in jagged shards of crockery.

He turned and pushed his way on down another
corridor, kicking through mounds of printed papers with
diagrams and pictures — manuals for the daily workings
of the platform. Then he saw the white door with a green
cross on it. Here was the medical bay. He pushed hard at

the door. It swung open, but inside the room was empty. Everything had been taken.

"No! No! NO!" cried Toby. He felt a hot rush of tears spring to his eyes and the knot of panic rose further in his throat. Someone had been here. Someone had beaten them to it. The cupboards had been torn from the walls and empty broken bottles littered the floor. Packets of Gamgee and lint dressings lay torn and discarded on the plastic chairs that sat lonely and unwanted in the large white room. He rushed to the medical cabinets with shattered glass doors but they were empty. All the medicines had been taken.

Toby stopped suddenly and listened. What was that? Was he imagining noises again? But as he stilled his breathing, he could just make out the faint boom of a foghorn coming from somewhere far below.

"Dad!" Toby cried and, turning on his heels, started to run back, stumbling over the piles of rubbish. But he couldn't remember the way he had come. All the corridors looked the same; every door led to another door that looked just the same as the last one. Toby felt the panic rising into his mouth now, threatening to choke him.

Think! Think! Be logical — there must be a main corridor with others leading off it. Just need to concentrate. Need to slow my breathing. Breathe — one elephant, two elephants ...

As he came round a corner Toby recognised the double doors of the canteen.

Not far now. Keep breathing!

He could still hear the distant *boom, boom* of the boat's foghorn sounding out into the mist below. There must be something wrong. What had his dad said about an emergency? Ah, the walkie-talkie!

Toby pulled it out of his cagoule pocket and frantically jabbed at the ON button. He put the walkie-talkie to his mouth.

"Dad! DAD!" he shouted into it. "What's happening?"

"Toby! Get back here now! Get back, Toby! NOW!" his dad screamed down the line.

2. Danger in the Mist

Toby staggered down the main corridor and out into the cold, clammy air. He ran down the walkway and lowered himself on to the ladder. The seagulls screeched and screamed abuse at him, angry at this invader in their territory. Slipping and sliding, he climbed down the ladder as fast as he could. He tried not to think of the pain in his hand or the height of the ladder above the cold North Sea. As he descended he caught glimpses of the bobbing boat below and of his dad, who stood on deck waving frantically to him.

"Toby! Hurry!" he screamed.

What did his dad think he was doing? Toby felt a stab of anger at his father. He was trying his hardest. Somehow it was never enough.

"Jump!" yelled his dad, as Toby got near the bottom of the ladder.

It's all right for you, thought Toby. *I'm the one hanging out over the sea.*

He jumped, throwing himself towards the boat deck. But as he came over the side of the boat, his foot trailed and caught on the lip of the bow. With a heavy thud he landed face down on the hard wooden deck.

"Ah!" he cried as his sore hand hit something solid.

"Shush!" His dad motioned him to be quiet. Toby strained to listen. All he could hear was the distant calling of the angry gulls, and the rhythmic slap of water on the side of the boat. He sat up and rubbed his sore knees.

Then, through the mist, he heard it: the unmistakable deep throb of an engine. It was no little fishing boat such as the *Lucky Lady*. It was a ship of some size and it was heading their way.

His dad returned to the wheelhouse, and pointed to the rope that still held them to the platform leg. Toby knew what to do.

Despite every muscle and sinew in his body aching and calling out for rest, he picked himself up. He took a long hooked pole from its bracket and, leaning over the bow, unhooked the rope from the spar. The wind was getting up and it took him a few efforts as the boat danced and sidled on the rising swell. At last he had the rope coiled and stowed back in the boat.

His dad reversed the boat from under the gigantic towers of the platform, and swung it away from the noise of the approaching ship.

Toby limped into the wheelhouse to join his dad.

"How big do you think it is?" he asked him.

"Difficult to tell in these conditions. The fog can amplify sounds. Certainly bigger than the *Lucky Lady* here," replied his dad.

The Lucky Lady? Huh! thought Toby. *We've had nothing but bad luck since we got her. Pity we can't change her name.* But his dad had said it was considered unlucky amongst the fisher folk to change the name of a boat.

His father slid the throttle handle forward and the boat picked up speed. "We need to get out of here," he said quietly, staring ahead.

"But Dad! It might not be pirates!" exclaimed Toby. "It might be good people, people who can help us. They might have medicine for Sylvie."

"It's not worth the risk, Toby," replied his dad.

Toby noticed his father's knuckles were white with clenching the steering wheel of the boat. His dad opened up the throttle some more. The *Lucky Lady*'s bow lifted as she picked up speed.

"Once they spot us on their radar we're a sitting duck.

They'll have an inflatable launched and reach us in minutes. And that will be the end of us."

"You don't know that! You can't run away from everybody we meet. At this rate we'll spend the rest of our lives on our own," cried Toby.

"Look, I'm sorry Tobes, but I just can't take the risk," said his dad. "Especially after what happened the last time we met another boat. That really scared me — that guy would have robbed us *and* thrown us all overboard if I hadn't forced him back into his own boat."

"That guy was a psycho ..." muttered Toby.

"And what's to say the guys in this ship aren't?" his dad replied. "We don't know what's out there, Toby. We don't know what's happened to the rest of the world. It could be in an even bigger mess than Scotland. Everyone is desperate now. Man is a selfish creature; do you think whoever they are would care that we have a sick child on board? Do you think they wouldn't take our fuel, our food and everything we've got if it would make their lives a little easier?" asked his dad.

Toby hadn't heard his dad say so much for ages, not since his mum had died. Usually he just barked orders at Toby, though sometimes at night when Toby lay in his tiny bunk bed in the stern, he could hear his dad singing a lullaby to Sylvie. It was one his mum had made up to sing to them both when they were babies. *Go to sleepy, little baby, go to slee-ee-py-byes ...*

Toby suddenly felt overcome with exhaustion. His body was crying out for sleep. He could see that there was no point in arguing with his dad — maybe he was right anyway.

"I'll go and check on Sylvie," he said quietly.

"Yep, you do that, Toby," his dad replied, without looking at him.

Toby paused, thinking that maybe his dad would ask him if he was OK after his disastrous mission.

"Oh, by the way," said Toby. "There was nothing left in the medical bay."

"Yeah, I'd already realised that," said his father.

"Somebody had been there and cleared the whole place out," Toby added.

"Yeah, well, even more reason for getting the hell out of here, in that case," remarked his dad.

"Yeah," sighed Toby.

Neither of them dared to acknowledge what this might mean for Sylvie.

Toby nursed his sore hand. He'd wrapped a dirty hankie round it but now the blood was beginning to ooze out. His dad hadn't noticed.

Toby left the wheelhouse and swung down the steps to the deck. Behind the wheelhouse was the deckhouse where they lived. Sylvie thought it looked cute with its shiny, varnished timber and smartly painted portholes in the sides. Toby heaved open the heavy steel door by the stiff awkward levers that sealed it tightly closed, making it watertight in a storm.

He wearily hung up his cagoule and pushed his way past the heaps of stuff stored in the narrow, cramped hallway. There were oilskins, bags of coal and logs for the stove, packs of loo paper, stacks of tinned soup and tuna, and a pile of wellies. He shuffled his feet out of his boots and into some dry trainers.

Inside the cabin hung the greasy smell of the previous day's dinner of fried corned beef and beans. A sharp pang in his stomach reminded Toby that that had been the last meal he'd eaten. There hadn't been time for breakfast that morning and, anyway, he would have been too nervous to eat it. He wondered if Sylvie had managed to eat anything that day.

Toby sighed as he picked up a dirty plastic tumbler from the table in the centre of the cabin, and threw it into the sink where the washing-up sat in slimy water. He glanced at the breadcrumbs and bean juice smeared across the table.

More chores to do. And all I want to do is sleep.

He picked up a soggy dishcloth and mopped half-heartedly at the sticky rings from beakers of juice. His dad would be cross if the table wasn't kept clean, as it was where he laid out his maps to plot their routes.

Toby smiled at the colourful ribbons Sylvie had tied to the brass rod which had been fitted round the table's edge to stop things sliding off it in a storm. When she felt well she was always making things out of the scraps of material Toby scrounged for her. He'd found the ribbons amongst some of his mum's belongings, after the accident.

Either side of the table were two bunk beds: one for his dad and one for Sylvie. Toby was thankful he didn't have to share the cramped space with the two of them. He liked the privacy of his own den, tucked cosily in the stern of the boat. It was the one place he could get away from this world of horror and madness.

"Hiya," he whispered into the pile of duvets and bedspreads that were heaped on top of Sylvie's bunk. A face appeared, with half-closed eyes wrinkling up at him.

"Tobes?" uttered a tiny sleepy voice.

"Who do you think it is? The Little Mermaid?" chuckled Toby.

More of Sylvie appeared: a mop of tousled blonde hair and a skinny white arm.

Too skinny, thought Toby. *She's wasting away in front of us.*

"I loved that film," said Sylvie, pushing herself up in the bed.

"The Little Mermaid?" asked Toby. "Yuk! That's for babies!" He laughed, pulling a strand of sticky blonde hair from in front of her eyes.

"Toby?" asked Sylvie. "Do you think we'll ever see that film again?"

"No, thank God!" replied Toby. "Now, if you want to watch a really good film, how about *Transformers Two*. That was brill!"

"But will we ever see a film again?"

Toby took Sylvie's small pale hand in his gnarled brown one.

"I honestly don't know, Sylvie," he said. "I just don't know what's going to happen. But don't you worry — Dad and I are on to it."

"Toby, what have you done to your hand?" gasped Sylvie. Toby had been hiding his injured hand behind him but Sylvie had spotted the blood-soaked hankie wrapped around it.

"It's nothing." Toby tried to shrug it off.

"Let me look," she asked.

"No! Don't make a fuss; it'll be fine," said Toby, pulling away his hand as she tried to inspect it.

"You should clean it before Dad sees it. You know what he's like about getting bugs and things."

"Yeah, yeah. Have you been asleep all morning?" he asked.

"Yes, I must've been," replied Sylvie, yawning. "Why are we moving so fast now?"

"Oh, no reason. Dad's in a hurry as usual, I suppose," replied Toby.

"Well, I'm still tired. I'm going to go back to sleep," she said. "Wake me up if you need me."

"Yep, I'll do that," said Toby, knowing that he wouldn't. There was nothing Sylvie could do any more to help him and his dad run the boat. She was weak as a kitten and spent most of the time sleeping.

Sylvie had been ill since their mum died. At first they'd thought she just had an infection, and the antibiotics they had stored at home seemed to be helping. But they'd run out. And now Sylvie was showing symptoms that they recognised all too well: a raging temperature, and a prickly red rash — all signs of the deadly red fever. Neither Toby nor his father had dared to speak their fears out loud.

Toby remembered Sylvie playing on the beach below the cottage at home. She liked to collect pebbles, especially the smooth white ones. She would caress them in her small grubby brown hands for hours, washing them in rock pools then drying them on a towel. Later she would carry them carefully, like treasure, up the rocky path to the back door. There, she would grade them into jam jars according to their size. Big ones in one jar. Little ones in another.

Toby preferred shells; they were more interesting. There were lots of different shapes and sizes and each one had a different pattern on its back. He would collect them by the carrier bag full and take them home to his mum. She loved shells too and would decorate the stone steps in the garden with them. She liked the fact that they weren't washed and still had sand and bits of sedge stuck to them. Toby remembered her smiling while she arranged the shells in patterns. He remembered that smile so well ...

Stop it! Toby told himself. That train of thought was bad. It led to a dark place, a place he didn't want to go.

Have to think of something else quick, he thought. *Pirates, yes, the pirates! I'd better go and see what's happening.*

With an effort, Toby pulled himself together and, after tucking Sylvie's blankets and covers around her, left the cabin.

3. Clever Pirates

Toby pulled on his oilskins and returned to the wheelhouse. The wind was picking up and the boat was getting tossed around as the waves grew higher and rougher. The *Lucky Lady*'s engine throbbed and juddered noisily as she strained against the battering sea.

Inside, it was quieter, except for the rhythmic *dub, dub* of the windscreen wipers as they cleared the spray that spattered over the front window. His dad stood staring stonily ahead, his hands still clenching the wheel.

"Sylvie's sleeping," Toby told him.

"Oh, good," replied his dad. "Best not to alarm her. I'm taking us north, up towards Inverness. If the pirates have picked us up on their radar and are following us, we may be able to lose them before we try to head home. Don't want to lead them straight back to Collieston."

"OK, Dad. But Sylvie's not looking great and I think the longer this trip is, the worse she'll get," replied Toby.

"Don't you think I know that?" his dad retorted angrily. "I'm just thinking of our safety. If they follow us home they'll find all our supplies. If we lose them, we'll starve. They're all we've got left."

Toby put his hand out to touch his dad's arm. "We'll find some more. We will. We just need to find medicine for Sylvie first and then we can go hunting for food again," said Toby.

His dad shrugged his hand away. "If only it was that easy," he remarked. "Have you forgotten the dogs?"

No, I haven't forgotten the dogs, thought Toby. *I was trying to be positive, like you always used to tell me to be. But positive thoughts don't seem to be helping much these days.*

How could he have forgotten the dogs? What a stupid thing for his dad to say. Wasn't it the dogs that had forced them to live their lives on this pathetic little fishing boat, trawling up and down the coast looking for food and fuel?

They couldn't travel freely on land any more. Pirates were a rare problem compared to the packs of wild dogs which now roamed the countryside, desperate for food. After their owners died, the dogs had soon grouped into packs in which only the biggest and strongest had survived. As time passed they were becoming more and more vicious and organised in their scavenging.

No, he couldn't forget the dogs. They were yet another nightmare to cope with in a world that had been turned upside down.

As the wind gusted and blew the mist away, the rugged outline of the Buchan coast came into view in the distance.

"I'm going to keep as close to the shoreline as possible. The *Lucky Lady* will be no match for a big ship in open waters. If the worst comes to the worst, we'll try and hide her in an inlet and make for safety on foot."

"What about the dogs? You know they've started to track boats from the shore," said Toby worriedly. "They might be there waiting for us."

"It's a risk we've got to take. We'll deal with that if and when it happens. At the moment my main worry is being followed by pirates," replied his dad. "Here, hold the wheel. Keep her steady," he said, motioning Toby to step up. His dad left the wheelhouse, picking up an old telescope on the way out. He was gone for what seemed like ages, then suddenly he burst back in.

"Here!" he said, thrusting the telescope at Toby. "I had a feeling we were being followed. See for yourself."

Toby took the cold brass telescope in his shaking

hands, and leapt down the steps to the deck. Gripping the handrail, he stumbled to the stern. Bracing his legs apart to hold himself steady, he lifted the instrument to his eye.

At first he could see nothing but angry foaming waves stretching for miles, but then he caught sight of the spiky outline of the oil platform. He wiped his hand across his face as the sea spray dripped from his hair down into his eyes.

I can't see anything. Dad's going mad! He's seeing things now!

He lifted the telescope once more to his eye, scrunching up his other eye to focus fully. There was the platform, slowly receding as the *Lucky Lady* ploughed gamely away from it.

"Oh no!" Toby exclaimed. There, sitting on the horizon, just to the right of the platform, was a ship. It wasn't a small fishing boat like theirs. It was a serious ship. Toby could see the ship's graceful lines and blue-grey colour, which told him it was a warship. There was no navy left; it had to be pirates.

Toby strained to keep the ship in vision, then suddenly a bright flash lit the side of the warship.

Boom! The sound of the gun firing hit Toby's ears seconds after the flash.

"DAD!" he shrieked. "They're firing at us!"

Just then he became aware of a loud whistling as

something flew through the air above the *Lucky Lady*. With a deafening roar the sea exploded in front of them as the shell hit the water. A towering plume cascaded over the decks, soaking Toby and throwing him to the floor.

The *Lucky Lady* swerved violently as his dad slewed the boat around the foaming waves, and set off in a different direction. Toby pulled himself back into the wheelhouse.

"Oh, Dad! That was near," he stuttered, shaking with cold and shock.

"That was just a warning shot — letting us know of their presence," his father said through gritted teeth. "They could have blown us out of the water if they'd wanted to."

"Shouldn't we stop and surrender?" gasped Toby.

"No way! They'll rob us and leave us with nothing. Perhaps we can lose them in this mist, if we just head for the coast. Take the wheel whilst I have a look at the map; I'm sure there's an inlet near here somewhere. Keep zigzagging — that'll stop them getting a bearing. Come on, get a move on."

Sometimes Toby wished his dad could just be a little nicer to him. He knew it was difficult for his dad, but things were difficult for them all. And it didn't look like they were going to get any better.

He shook his damp hair out of his eyes and took the wheel, trying to concentrate on holding the boat on its course. Maybe his dad's plan would work — just to keep going as fast as they could and hope they lost the pirates in the mist, or maybe the pirates would lose interest in them. At that moment, neither of those seemed very likely. After all, they were pitting the poor old *Lucky Lady* against a warship.

And as for losing interest — what else had the pirates to do with their time? It wasn't as if there was a lot of traffic in these seas. Toby and his dad had only come across a couple of boats in the two years they'd been sailing along this coastline.

The *Lucky Lady* bobbed choppily over the water as Toby concentrated on steering her right and then left, all the time heading for the thin dark line of the mainland glimpsed through the mist. The rough motion of the boat bouncing up and down on the waves no longer bothered Toby. When they had first taken trips away in the boat, in search of food and provisions, they had all been very sick. Even his dad had succumbed to seasickness, despite having been a weekend sailor all his life.

Toby had never liked sailing. He had refused to get into his dad's dinghy from a young age. Looking back now, he couldn't think why he had made such a fuss about it. Maybe that was why his dad was mean to him.

Toby didn't think so. He knew the real reason. His dad blamed him for his mum's death; he was sure of that now. It had been an accident, but there was nothing more he could do to convince his father that it wasn't his fault. And, anyway, it hadn't always been like it was now. He could remember his dad playing footie on the beach with him, laughing and shouting at his mum to join in. She would sit with her knitting, a beanie hat pulled over her fair hair, watching over baby Sylvie in her wicker Moses basket. Toby still had that beanie hat. It was tucked away with the rest of his treasures in a box in his cubbyhole under the stern.

Toby yawned. He needed to sleep. His legs and arms felt leaden with exhaustion.

His dad burst back in, shaking the water from his oilskin jacket. "Getting a bit rough out there," he remarked. "I've checked the map: if we head due north by north-west, it shouldn't take long to get to the caves near the Bullers of Buchan. I know that area; it shouldn't be difficult to find a cave big enough to hide *Lady* in. We've got to try — it's our only chance."

Toby nodded, his brain fuzzy with tiredness. He could let his dad take over — now he had a plan.

"Can you get something for Sylvie to eat? She needs to keep her strength up," said his dad gruffly. "Then come back; I need you here to help. We both have to stay alert, calm and focused, otherwise we'll not get out of this alive." He came over and took the wheel.

"Yep, of course," said Toby. "I'll make Sylvie some noodles. She used to like those. We've still got a whole case of them left."

He tiredly made his way round to the deckhouse, trying not to look to the horizon. He didn't want to see how close the pirates were. Better not to know. Then he could look at Sylvie without the terror of pursuit in his face. But it was difficult not to think about what they might do next. Would they fire on them again? Only next time it might not be a warning shot …

4. Survival of the Fittest

"Sylvie?" called Toby, entering the cosy warmth of the cabin. He'd brought in a couple of logs from the lobby and, carefully opening the door of the small pot-belly stove, popped them in. The stove was their only source of heat in the cabin, and it was his job to make sure it didn't go out. From Sylvie's hump of blankets, came a muffled sob.

"Sylvie? You all right?" he asked, going over to the bunk.

There was another little yelp.

He pulled back the layers of duvets and blankets to reveal a wild-eyed Sylvie, creased and crumpled with sleep. She grabbed at his arm.

"Toby! Oh, Toby!" she cried. "I was alone on the

boat and I called for you and Dad and Mum but nobody came! And something else was here. I could hear it growling and snapping above deck. I could hear its claws scratching at the door of the cabin. And it forced the door open and then I could see it was a huge black dog. It was slobbering, Toby. It was going to eat me!"

Toby took Sylvie into his arms and held her tight.

"It's all right, Sylvie, I'm here. It was just a nightmare," he told her. "It's OK, Dad and I are here. The dogs can't get on to the boat; you know that. They can't get us here." He soothed her, stroking her matted blonde hair with his sore hand, the bloodstained hankie still tied around it.

"Oh, Tobes! It was SO real! I opened my mouth to scream but I couldn't. It was horrible. I was going to die!" she exclaimed.

"It's OK, Sylvie, you're not going to die. Dad and I are here to protect you. Nothing bad is going to happen. D'you hear me?" he said, pushing her backwards so she could see his face. "Nothing is going to hurt you, d'you understand?"

She stared with wide frightened eyes into his, clinging hard on to him.

"Now, let's calm down," said Toby, trying to feel in control, but it was difficult, knowing the dangerous situation they were presently in. He wished he believed what he had told her — that everything was OK, that nothing was going to hurt her. But the truth was, he just didn't know what was going to happen.

"Hey, why don't we get Henry out to play?" he suggested. "He always cheers you up, doesn't he?"

Sylvie rubbed her tear-stained face with the sleeve of her pyjamas, and tried hard to smile.

"Yeah, let's get him out. He's not been out for ages," she replied.

Toby went into the utility area on the other side of the stove. There was a shower cubicle and toilet in a narrow corridor, and another door that led on deck. In the corner, by the shower, balanced on crates of bottled water, was a small plastic hutch where Henry lived. Toby opened the hutch door carefully and pulled out the furry bundle that was Henry. Cradling him in his arms, he took the rabbit through to Sylvie.

"Here," he said, "make a lap for him." Toby gently lifted the rabbit from his arms and placed it into the folds of the blankets on Sylvie's knees.

The tawny brown rabbit wrinkled his small black nose at them and stared around. He looked comical with his large floppy ears drooping down each side of his head.

"Hello, Henry," said Sylvie, smiling broadly. "How are you today?"

"Did you manage to get up and feed him earlier?" Toby asked.

"Yes, I would never let Henry go hungry no matter how poorly I felt," said Sylvie indignantly.

"Good. I don't suppose you felt well enough to muck him out, though?"

"Oops, sorry, Tobes, I forgot," replied Sylvie.

Toby wearily went back out to the corridor and started to clean out the hutch. What could he say? Sylvie was sick and he was a lot older — six years to be precise. As such, he felt he had to help his dad shoulder some of the responsibilities. Cleaning out a rabbit hutch wasn't such a big deal, was it? Compared to the pirates on their tail!

Toby stopped to listen to the pulsating sound of the *Lucky Lady*'s engine, coming from down below in the engine room. She seemed to have developed a high-pitched whine along with all the usual engine noises.

Oh great, that's all we need to happen — engine failure! We'll be like a sitting duck, as Dad says. Maybe I should go and tell him the engine's not sounding too good?

Toby paused and thought about his dad's likely reaction. He wouldn't be too pleased, and what was the point of adding another worry?

After all, I might be imagining it — stress can do funny things to you …

Toby went back into the cabin, where Sylvie sat calmly stroking Henry and chattering away to the rabbit, who was happily chewing a tassel on the bedspread.

Toby went to put on the gas cooker at the back of the cabin. They had managed to find several large canisters of gas on an earlier foraging trip. An old croft down by the shore front, near Balmedie beach, had for some reason been full of them. Cooking on the solid fuel stove was tiresome and took ages. Toby much preferred the cooker, even though it meant him and his dad had had to lug the heavy canisters from the croft across the sands and down to the mooring, where they had struggled to lift them on to the *Lucky Lady*. It felt worth all that effort when they sat down to a hot meal together.

He made some noodles for Sylvie, boiling them up in a pan on the hob, and sprinkling the sachet of disgusting-smelling powder on to the wriggling white tubes. She had loved the sticky pasta when she was younger, and had eaten nothing else for months before their mum died. But since then she had eaten less and less.

Toby handed Sylvie the bowl of noodles.

"D'you want something with that? Might be able to rustle you up a wee drop of Heinz tomato ketchup. This is a classy restaurant. We only have the best here!"

Sylvie smiled and took the bowl, sniffing at its contents.

"And don't go feeding it to that blinking rabbit, either," Toby gently teased.

"No, sir!" replied Sylvie.

"I'm just going to have a quick nap. I'm knackered," sighed Toby, lying down on his dad's bunk. It smelt of his dad: a warm manly smell of old sweat mixed with diesel oil. Toby fell asleep before he heard Sylvie's reply.

Toby woke with a start. Something was wrong. What was it?

The engine had stopped. The *Lucky Lady* was no longer powering forwards through the waves. She was sitting silently, bobbing in the choppy waters.

Suddenly his dad burst through the cabin door.

"Toby!" he shouted. "Come quickly! I need your help — the fuel line must be blocked. The engine's stalled and I can't restart it. Come on! Don't just lie there!"

Toby swung his legs down over the bunk sides and stood up, rubbing the sleepy dust from his eyes. He felt like he'd been kicked by a mule.

"Er … yeah, Dad, I'm coming. Oh, my head's so sore." Toby rubbed his head with his good hand. The sore hand was too swollen to touch anything.

"It's cold in here," remarked his dad, moving over to Sylvie to tuck her in. She was fast asleep with Henry, fast asleep too, tucked under her chin. "Can't I even trust you to keep the fire in the stove? You know that's your job."

"I did … I put some logs on earlier …" stuttered Toby, but he knew there was no point in saying anything. As far as his dad was concerned, he had let him down again. "Sorry …" Toby mumbled.

"Come on, get the stove cracking and then come up on deck and keep watch whilst I try to fix the fuel line," commanded his dad. "That last lot of diesel we got from the croft in Balmedie must have been dirty. Some rubbish or other is bunging up the fuel line." His dad bent over Sylvie, kissed her gently on the top of her head, and then left, yelling, "And put that darned rabbit back in its box while you're at it!"

Within five minutes Toby had followed all his dad's orders and joined him on the deck. The evening had crept up on them whilst he'd been sleeping and now the only light was the spotlight that hung off the deckhouse wall. It threw an eerie puddle of yellow on to the sea, which looked black and menacing in the darkness.

"Have we lost the pirates?" Toby asked his dad anxiously.

"Can't be sure one way or the other. I can't see anything out there but the wind has dropped again and there are banks of fog rolling in and out along the coastline just now, so they could easily be quite near us and we'd never know until they ran us down," replied his dad.

"That doesn't sound too cheery," said Toby. "And now we've got engine problems. Great!"

"I might be able to fix the engine if it's what I think it is," said his dad, "but you need to keep an eye out for any lights, and listen carefully. You'll be able to hear an outboard on an inflatable boat for miles. My guess is they won't want to bring the warship too near this coast. It's too rocky and dangerous for a big boat. No, I'm sure they'll launch an attack by dinghy."

His dad disappeared into the deckhouse and Toby could hear him descending the steep steps down to the engine room under the cabin. Toby decided to check the rope and anchor that were keeping them steady. His dad wouldn't be pleased if there was too much movement when he was carrying out the delicate job of removing, cleaning and restoring the fuel line to the engine.

He went to the stern and tugged at the rope. Good, the boat felt firmly anchored, now all he had to do was keep a lookout.

Toby stood and stared out into the inky blackness of the night. How lonely it felt to be in the middle of the ocean when danger was just around the corner. Now there were no emergency services you could pick up the phone to and ring. There was no one to save you from the bad guys — no army, no police, not even paramedics or doctors. They had been the first to go when the red fever had swept like a bush fire across the world. Toby could understand why the doctors soon succumbed to the infection; after all, they were looking after the first wave of sick people that flooded the hospitals.

But the army and the navy and air forces? How come they didn't withstand the onslaught? You'd think they would have had procedures in place to protect them from things like a virus. Toby had seen lots of films in which soldiers ran around in protective suits with breathing apparatus on, maintaining some degree of law and order. They were the ones that stopped civilisation imploding into mass panic and mob rule.

Without laws and people to enforce them, would mankind revert to behaving like animals? The survival of the fittest. Toby had learnt that theory at school. Wasn't it Darwin who first put it forward? He couldn't remember, but what did it matter now? The fittest had survived, and on land that had turned out to be the dogs.

Ha! thought Toby. *They must be laughing now, after all those centuries of doing man's bidding: fetching stupid balls and chasing sticks, rounding up sheep and digging out lost climbers. The boot is on the other paw now!*

"Toby!" His dad's shout jolted him from his wandering thoughts.

"Yes?" he replied.

"Can you go into my small tool bag in the wheelhouse and bring me an adjustable spanner?"

"Going!" Toby sped as fast as he could to find the tool

his father wanted, returning with it clasped in his hand. "Here you are …" He held it out to his dad who had surfaced from the engine room, wiping his oily hands on a rag.

"D'you hear that?" said his dad in a quiet voice. "Listen."

Toby stopped in his tracks and listened.

There it was — the distant rising and falling whine of an outboard motor attached to an inflatable dinghy that was bouncing off and on the waves.

His father flung himself at the light switch for the deck light and they were plunged into darkness.

"They're coming!" his dad whispered fiercely. "We must hide!"

"Hide? Where? It won't take long to find us on this little boat," Toby whispered back.

"Not us! Hide the *Lucky Lady*! We must hide her!" said his dad, turning to release the anchor rope and tugging up the anchor.

"Where?" asked Toby.

"I stopped here for a reason. We're near the Bullers of Buchan. There are loads of caves around here. We just need to get her into one."

"Dad, the Bullers of Buchan — isn't that a very dangerous bit of rocky shore for a boat to be near, especially in the dark?"

"All the better then — the pirates won't want to risk it."

"And how are we going to get her into a cave?"

"You steer her, and I'll use the dinghy to pull her. I won't use the outboard motor; I'll row. I don't want them to hear us. The tide's coming in; she'll only need guiding once we get going."

"You sure about this?" Toby asked anxiously.

"Toby, we've no choice. Now let's get on with it." With that, his dad hoisted himself over the side and into the small rubber dinghy which sat tied at the back of the *Lucky Lady*.

OK, Toby, time to focus. Go to the wheelhouse and steer. That's all you have to do. It's that easy. Now go! His heart was thumping loudly as he pulled himself up the steps and into the wheelhouse.

5. Hide and Seek

Standing in the wheelhouse with his hands on the wheel, Toby didn't feel tired any more. He felt as if someone had peeled back his skin and exposed every nerve in his body. Every sinew felt taut and wired, as if he was about to go twang like an overstretched guitar string.

He concentrated his mind on the task. He must help his dad steer the boat to safety. A calmness came over him and he knew what he had to do.

The boat lurched forward as he felt a slight tug on the bow. *That must be Dad.*

Toby swung the wheel over to the left, pointing the bow in the direction that the tug came from.

His dad must have taken compass readings; he must know what direction to row in order to reach the Bullers of Buchan. But how far were they from the huge granite towers that arched from the jagged shore?

Toby remembered childhood picnics on the grassy tops of the cliffs there. He and Sylvie had lain on their bellies to crane their necks over the lip of the precipice, and watched the screaming gulls, cormorants, shags and guillemots wheeling and diving from their nests. The din was unbelievable as thousands of birds screeched and squawked at one another, each defending their territory. Toby had pointed out to Sylvie the squat puffins with their funny striped faces, perched higher up on tiny ledges. Monty, their collie, had had to stay in the car, as Toby's mum had been scared he would chase the birds and fall over the edge.

The boat suddenly lurched forward again — another tug on the bow. His dad must be a lot stronger than Toby had thought. Slowly the *Lucky Lady* began to move forwards, dipping gracefully into the black waters.

Toby kept his eyes straining ahead. He could make out nothing in the dark, but he'd left the doors to the wheelhouse open so that he could hear if his dad shouted any instructions.

The *Lucky Lady*'s progress was slow and painful. Toby daren't step outside to look behind in case he saw the pirates catching up. The only noises were the slow breaking of the waves on the sides of the boat, and the occasional grunt from his father as he leant all his weight on the oars of the little dinghy. Maybe the pirates had got lost in the fog and turned round and gone back to the warship.

The boat glided on. Toby could now hear the sound of waves crashing on rocks. These were treacherous waters, with hidden rocks and boulders under the water, and the pull and swirl of a rising tide to fight. Toby felt his hands sticky with sweat against the warm wood of the wheel. Surely his dad wouldn't attempt this without knowing these waters? Perhaps as a teenager he had fished here from his sailing dinghy? Perhaps when his parents were young, they had spent Sundays exploring the caves along this coast? Toby fervently hoped so.

Just then he had the feeling of a shadow passing over the boat, and the world suddenly got darker. They were passing under an overhanging piece of cliff and into a cave. The left-hand side of the boat thudded into something solid and immovable.

"Drop anchor!" his dad shouted hoarsely.

Toby ran to the stern and, picking up the heavy iron anchor, threw it into the water.

The boat skidded along the cave wall to a halt. His father appeared at the stern.

"Not bad for an old sailor, eh?" he said. Toby could feel his dad's smile in the dark. It had been some feat of sailing.

Toby sighed with relief. He couldn't believe his dad had just towed a fishing boat into a cave in the dark. Toby wanted to reach out and hug him, to put his arms around him and say, "Thank you, Dad!" But somehow he couldn't. Because he knew what his dad's response would be. It would be what it always was when Toby tried to get close to him. Rejection.

Instead, Toby got on with busying himself, coiling up the spare anchor rope, checking the dinghy was tied up. It was difficult in the dark but a weak moon was peeping through a band of cloud, throwing a milky white light into the cave. He could just make out the outline of things on the deck. His dad sat rubbing his arms and stretching his neck muscles as if he was sore.

They both heard it at the same time. This time the noise of the motor was accompanied by the sound of men's voices — deep, gruff voices, shouting out into the night.

"Where've they gone? I'm sure they came this way," came one voice.

"Get a bit further in, Jim," came another.

They were getting nearer.

Toby dropped to his knees and, crouching low, made his way to his dad, who was now lying down in the prow, peering over the front of the boat.

His father motioned with his finger to his mouth for Toby to keep quiet.

They both listened and waited.

"They couldn't have steered that boat into these caves; they'd be barmy — the rocks are far too dangerous," yelled Jim.

"Capt'n said not to come back without them," barked another voice. "He was well mad — blighters making off like that. Lucky for them our radar was out. We'd have had 'em no bother. One shot to the rudder and they'd have been ours."

As the sounds came closer, the mouth of the cave was lit with a dancing spotlight from the pirates' craft.

Toby grabbed his dad's arm and clung on to it. His dad for once left it there. Toby felt both his and his father's breath stop, as if by not breathing they could make themselves disappear.

The light swept across the first ten metres of the overhang but then swept away again. Toby and his dad quickly lowered their heads under the parapet of the prow so they could only hear what was going on.

"Nah, there's nothing here. We can't take 'em back if they're not here, can we?" an angry voice called out.

"Time to get back to the ship, eh?" said Jim

"Aye, about time," the second voice agreed.

The whine of the outboard dropped to a *chug, chug* noise and then there was silence.

The walls of the cave echoed with the gruff voices of

the three men in the dinghy as it sat just outside the cave, blocking the moonlight.

"Are you sure you checked good and proper?" yelled a new voice.

"Aye, nothing there, pal. Let's head back to the ship," said Jim.

The shouts fell to a grumble, and they heard someone trying to start the motor again. Toby heard the pull of the cord ripping the engine into life. It stuttered and failed.

Don't say we're going to be trapped in here with them adrift out there, thought Toby.

"Toby? What's happening? What's all the noise?"

Toby turned towards the voice. It was coming from the door of the deckhouse. It was Sylvie. Toby didn't have time to think what to do. He just did it.

He threw himself down the boat on his stomach, sliding down the wet deck on his front, slithering to a halt at Sylvie's feet. He half rose and then rugby-tackled her around the legs, pulling her down towards him.

As she hit the deck, he placed his hankie-wrapped hand over her mouth and forced it shut. There he lay, half on top of her, half choking her, while she writhed and tried to scream underneath him.

Toby heard the men's voices raised once more. Had they heard Sylvie?

"Sylvie!" he whispered frantically in her ear. "Sylvie,

stop struggling! You must keep quiet now! Our lives depend on it, Sylvie."

As she stopped struggling and went limp underneath him, he relaxed the hold on her mouth. He felt her spit out the blood-tasting cotton of the hankie. At that moment the pirates' motor sprang into life. The dinghy accelerated fast away from the mouth of the cave. They were gone.

"Sorry, Sylvie. Are you all right? I didn't hurt you, did I?" Toby crouched over the rag-doll form of his sister on the deck. She didn't move.

"Sylvie?" His dad had joined him and was bending over the still body. In one movement he scooped her up into his arms and swung through the door of the deckhouse. Toby followed him into the cabin.

"Is she OK, Dad?" asked Toby, his voice cracking with concern.

His father didn't reply. He gently laid Sylvie on the pile of blankets and pulled some around her.

"I'm really sorry …" stuttered Toby. "I didn't mean to hurt her. I didn't think, I was just trying to …"

His dad looked at him. "You did the right thing, Toby. If they'd heard her we might all be dead by now. She's probably shocked more than anything. Did she bang her head?"

"I can't remember. It all happened so fast," Toby

replied. He sat down on the edge of Sylvie's bed and took hold of her small white hand that was drooping over the side.

"Sylvie? Talk to me, Sylve," he begged, sniffing back tears.

"You sit here and keep an eye on her," said his Dad. "We can't stay here long; they may be back. I need to get on with fixing that fuel line. If I rig the spotlight up in the engine room, no one should see it from outside the cave. But we need to be gone before daylight in case they come back for a closer look."

Toby nodded. How could his dad be so calm with Sylvie lying unconscious on the bed? How could he get on with things as if nothing had happened? What if Sylvie didn't wake up? What then?

Toby felt red-hot tears trickling down his grimy face. He hated crying. That was for girls. He hadn't cried since his mum died. There wasn't time for all that emotional stuff. You only got all choked up with tears and snot and your eyes went sore and gritty and red. Then people knew you'd been crying, and you didn't want anyone to see that.

Toby wiped the filthy hankie on his hand across his dirt-streaked face and sniffed loudly.

Come on, Sylvie. Come on and wake up for your Tobes. PLEASE.

He willed her to wake up, but the pale face lying on the pillow showed no sign of life. The only way he knew she was still alive was by the shallow rise and fall of her skinny chest inside the pink fluffy pyjamas.

He pulled the duvet up close round her neck. Her hand felt cold. Toby decided to stoke the stove to warm up the cabin. Had he read somewhere that a person in shock could die from loss of body heat? He went to the lobby to fetch some logs to build up a good fire. After he had got a blaze going he went to get Sylvie a bottle of water. Had he also read that dehydration could be a problem? But how was he going to get her to drink when she was unconscious?

"Hiya, Henry," he greeted the fluffy rabbit who was sitting cleaning himself in his hutch on top of the bottles of water.

Ah, thought Toby, *I remember hearing that someone in a hospital somewhere was once woken up by a famous footballer talking to them, even though they had been in a coma for months. I wonder if Henry could work his usual magic?*

Excitedly, Toby pulled the surprised rabbit from his hutch.

"Come on, Henry. You've got a job to do." Toby took the rabbit and laid him carefully on the bed next to Sylvie. Then he took her hand and, holding it gently, stroked Henry's soft fur. Nothing happened at first but

Toby kept on going. Then he started to sing the lullaby that his mum had made up for them.

"Go to sleepy, go to sleepy, go to slee-ee-py-byes ..."

I don't know why I'm singing a lullaby. I want her to wake up, not go to sleep!

But he found singing the lullaby, his mum's lullaby, to be soothing. He felt the tensions of the night slipping away. He would have loved to crawl into his own little nest and drift into a peaceful sleep. His eyes grew heavy and the words of the song became slower and slower until ...

"Dad? Is that you?" A wee voice mumbled from the pillow.

"No, it's Toby. I'm right beside you, Sylvie."

"Was that you singing?" the sleepy voice asked. "I've never heard you singing that song before, Tobes."

"No? Well, I'm not a good singer, that's why. Not nearly as good as Mu— Look, Sylvie, I've brought Henry to see you."

Sylvie propped herself up on one elbow and smiled at the sight of the small rabbit sitting up on his back legs, busily washing his ears.

"What happened?" she asked, rubbing the back of her head. "I've got a bump. Feel it." She stuck her head towards Toby to feel. He rubbed his hand gingerly over it.

"Yep! You've got a right lump there. It's the size of an egg!" he joked.

"So how did I get that?" she quizzed.

"Oh, it was my fault. I was playing too rough on the deck and knocked you down by accident. But you're OK now, aren't you?"

"Yeah, I just feel a little sore, but y'know what? I'm really hungry!" said Sylvie.

"Great! I'll make us some dinner." Toby smiled with intense relief.

6. The Boat Graveyard

Toby was woken by his dad shaking him. "Toby!" he hissed in his ear. "Wake up! It's your turn to keep watch. I must get some sleep. Wake me up at three; we need to get going before the sun comes up. We're not far from Peterhead here. We must try and get into the harbour before daylight."

"Huh?" Toby sat up and rubbed his eyes. He had fallen asleep on his dad's bunk after eating a dinner of porridge, crackers and peanut butter.

"Come on, up you get," commanded his dad. "I've cleaned out and fixed the fuel line, but I can't take the risk of using that diesel again. It's dirty. I've found a small can of clean fuel but it's only enough to get us into Peterhead. We must look for more fuel there."

"Isn't that risky?" asked Toby, pulling on a thick jumper.

"We've no choice," stated his dad. "Now, don't forget, set your alarm for three AM."

Toby nodded and sleepily went through to the lobby to put on his oilskins. Up on deck it was eerily dark and still. A bank of fog had rolled in and the air in the cave hung heavy with dampness. A disgusting smell of rotting seaweed filled Toby's nostrils and he gagged as he took a deep breath.

He made his way to the bow where his dad had spread an old tarpaulin on which to sit and keep watch. Toby sat down and pulled it around himself. Keeping watch was the worst duty on the boat. He had to keep awake with nothing to do but stare at the black water licking at the sides of the boat, and listen to the constant *drip, drip, drip* of water falling from the wet roof of the cave. He could vaguely make out the entrance to the cave, where the waves picked up and crashed against the rocky hole. He snuggled down and tried to think of something positive that would keep him awake.

I need to invent something. What about an alarm that's triggered by the scent of a dog? That would be useful. Would have to work from batteries though. No, that's no good. We've almost run out of batteries and we might never find any more. What we really need is a wind turbine to generate electricity without fuel. Our old generator uses far too much diesel and we might be short of that soon. Yes, a wind turbine, that's what we need …

Toby remembered how his mum had fought the development of wind farms near their village. She was really scary when she got fired up about something she felt strongly about. Toby smiled to himself. He had felt so proud of his mum. She'd been so brave to stand up to "those suits" as she called them. She wasn't like the other boys' mums at school. She was …

NO! How many times must I say this? Toby told himself. *Don't go there! It hurts!*

Toby tried to concentrate on the design of the wind turbine. They would need some metal posting, something to make blades out of, and …

The *drip, drip, drip* of the water in the cave filled his head, and he felt it getting heavier and heavier.

Must stay awake, mustn't fall …

The black dog was massive. It stood in front of him, a thick stream of slobber drooling from its open jaws. Toby could see the sharp teeth glinting in the blood-red lining of its enormous mouth. It was staring straight at him. Its eyes had a curious opaque look to them, giving the dog an air of other-worldliness. The thick black hairs on its shoulders were standing up, making the dog look even bigger and more ferocious. It was growling, a low angry vibration coming from deep within its chest.

"Don't come near my family!" Toby heard his mum's voice say. "Go, and don't return here!" she commanded the dog.

But it didn't move; it was watching Toby with those pale, unblinking eyes.

"Run, Toby! Run!" his mum shouted. He couldn't see her; he could only see the dog. "Run!" she screamed.

But Toby couldn't move his feet. They were stuck in glue.

The dog started to advance slowly, foam and spit flying through the air as it turned its huge head from side to side.

Toby could smell its foul, pungent breath. He tried to move his arms but they, too, were stuck to his sides.

The beast got nearer and nearer. Toby opened his mouth to scream but nothing came out ...

"Toby! What did I tell you?" It was his dad's voice, shouting at him. "Can't I trust you to do anything? You were supposed to wake me an hour ago!"

"What?" mumbled Toby. "Have they gone? The dogs? Where am I?"

"Toby, you've been having bad dreams again. You fell asleep."

"Sorry, Dad, the alarm can't have gone off."

"Well, it would help if you had set it in the first place!" His dad shoved the alarm clock under Toby's nose. "See — you forgot to wind it up!"

"Sorry, Dad, I ..." Toby could say nothing. He knew it was his fault. He had forgotten all about the alarm.

"And as for falling asleep on watch. Come on, Toby! I can't do everything all the time!" His dad stormed off to pick up the anchor.

There was a stony silence between them as they set about preparing the boat for the next leg of their journey. Toby battened down the loose hatches and tidied away ropes and tools. The boat was ready just as the water in the cave started to turn a rich pinkie-red from the sun slowly emerging over the horizon. The fog had cleared and the day promised to be clear and sunny. There was no sign of the pirates from the night before. Toby hoped they were still sleeping. The early morning sea air was cold and crisp, biting against Toby's face in a slight breeze as the *Lucky Lady* scraped carefully through the cave mouth and on to the open seas.

They couldn't travel too fast. The small amount of fuel they had left would be enough for them to crawl around the jagged coastline at the Bullers of Buchan, past the long-since derelict RAF station near Boddam and the tumbling-down power station that stood on the headland near Peterhead. Once in the harbour they would have to find more fuel.

Toby felt bad. He had let his dad down again. He had let himself and Sylvie down too. It was the worst sin ever to fall asleep on duty. All sailors knew that. In the old days he would have been made to walk the plank, shot or thrown overboard. Toby tried to think of a way to make it up to his dad but nothing came into his head. Perhaps he should just keep quiet and get on with his jobs.

He went below and saw to Sylvie, getting her a bowl of hot water so that she could have a wash, and fetching her toothbrush and toothpaste. He cleaned out Henry's hutch, rinsed the chemical toilet and changed the sheets on Sylvie's bed. Then he washed up the pots left lying in the sink, wiped down the table and gave Sylvie a beaker of juice. He still felt bad, but at least all the chores were done now.

"Toby! Come and look!" His dad was calling him from above deck. Toby went to see what it was.

"Look, Tobes." He sounded in a better mood. The sun was bouncing off the dancing waves, reflecting the bright light upwards, making it difficult to see in the wheelhouse. His dad had his favourite aviator shades on. He turned to smile at Toby.

"Up there is Peterhead prison," he said, pointing to the top of a cliff as they rounded the headland. "In the nineteenth century, the prisoners were made to build those magnificent breakwaters out of granite blocks. Can you imagine that? Look at the size of those breakwaters." He pointed ahead to where two tall, long walls stuck out into the sea, creating an enormous sheltered area for ships to anchor.

"They didn't have diggers or cranes in those days. It would have been all horse and cart for transport and then just hard physical labour." His dad paused, thoughtfully.

Toby squinted up at the tall bleak prison sitting high above them. Dark shadows were flitting across the base of its white walls. "Dogs," he muttered uneasily. "There are dogs watching us." After last night's dream, they were the last thing he wanted to see.

"We'll be all right once we're in the harbour. There's a ten foot security fence; they won't get over that in a hurry," reassured his father. "That's if it hasn't corroded and fallen down. It's like everything else, Toby — there's no one left to look after anything. I mean, who's going to maintain the breakwaters now?"

The good mood had gone as quickly as it had come.

Toby glanced at his dad, he couldn't see his eyes, hidden as they were by the dark glasses. "It'll get better, Dad. We've got to believe that, or else …"

"Yeah, I know." His father tried hard to sound cheery. "Bit of a thought, though, eh? Everything we've ever known — roads, cities, harbours — all left to just fall into decay ..." He coughed and turned away.

Toby decided to leave his dad to do his emotional stuff on his own. But as he turned to leave, his dad placed his hand on his sleeve. "Give us a hand tying up, will you, Tobes?"

Toby nodded and stood quietly at his father's side as the *Lucky Lady* sailed into Peterhead harbour.

The main sheltered area that lay in the massive arms of the north and south breakwaters was for the really big ships that needed deep anchorage. Two of these were still tied up to the north wall, their bright red paint faded and rusted to a strange pale pink colour. As the diminutive *Lucky Lady* chugged on by, Toby could make out the names of the ships, *Seven Seas* and *Seven Atlantic,* painted on their bows, which towered above him.

Toby wondered if there had been many more ships here during the epidemic. Had the men on them all become sick at the same time, and the ships had to limp into harbour with a dying crew on board? Or had the men decided that they needed to get home to their loved ones before they all got sick and died? What had happened to the rest of the ships?

Most likely got smashed up by storms, thought Toby. *Once the mooring chains broke, even a big ship would be swept away by the sort of storms the north-east has in winter. There must loads of wrecks up and down the coast.*

Toby and his dad had only seen one wreck. That had been at Balmedie beach, not far down the coast from their village. The shipwreck had sat upright on the long expanse of sand like a huge metal dog waiting for someone to throw it a stick into the sea. They had climbed on it. It had still been safe in those days to go on the beach. They couldn't go there any more. The dogs would get them.

Sailing on through the outer harbour, they were channelled by the walls of the inner harbour into a smaller area. They didn't get far. The fishing harbour was a graveyard of boats, big and little. It looked like a giant hand had scooped up all the boats and thrown them up into the air to land higgledy-piggledy back into the basin of the harbour. Everywhere there were boats thrown topsy-turvy all over the place. Boats sat on top of other boats, boats leant drunkenly against each other as if, like dominoes, one push and they would all fall over. There were old fishing boats, like the *Lucky Lady*, in many sizes and shapes — some modern, some old-fashioned. There were pleasure boats, large fibreglass-hulled catamarans, gin palaces with sun decks, and speedboats with huge outboard motors at their sterns. Toby had never seen so many different types and sizes of boats in his life.

"Why haven't we been here before?" he asked his dad. "This is amazing! We could have got ourselves a much better boat than the poor old *Lucky Lady* here."

"Yeah, I suppose so," replied his dad. "But, anyway, the *Lucky Lady* has been good to us. We were lucky to find her — just sitting there on her own in that tiny harbour at Newburgh. D'you remember?"

"Yeah, how could I forget? She was full of rats. Lucky we still had Monty then. He made short work of them!" Toby laughed. His dad's mood had swung upbeat again. The early summer sunshine warming their backs was making them both feel better.

"Right, let's go and find some fuel. I've got the siphon. It'll be nice to get home tonight and have a proper sleep for a change," remarked his dad, swinging the boat slowly over to the quayside. "Actually, you'd better stay here and keep an eye on Sylvie. We don't want her waking up and panicking," said his dad, leaping from the deck on to a rusted ladder on the wall of the quay. "Hand me those jerrycans, can you, Tobes?"

"D'you think we're safe here?" Toby asked as he passed up the metal jerrycans to his dad on the quay.

"What? Oh, I should think they've moved on by now. Pirates don't hang around as a rule," replied his dad.

"You think?" said Toby. "I wouldn't think you could apply rules to pirates."

"Keep your eye open for anything, just in case. This place gives me the creeps," said his dad, setting off towards the harbour depot carrying four of the jerrycans.

A small, dishevelled, pyjama-clad person appeared on deck. She looked hot and clammy as she stood scratching at a red blotchy rash which was spreading up from her neck and across her face. Toby gulped.

"Are you OK, Sylvie? Coming sunbathing?" he called to her from the wheelhouse.

"It's really hot down there," said Sylvie. "I need some fresh air … Poo!" she cried. "It really pongs out here!" She sat down shakily on a metal storage box in the bow.

"Don't worry, you soon get used to it," remarked Toby. Filling the air was a rich odour of oil-stained water, decaying fish spoil, litter and the odd dead seagull. As the sun baked down the smell intensified, and a hazy layer of putrefying gas hung over the oily patches in the harbour waters.

"I'll go and get you a rug to sit on," said Toby, disappearing into the deckhouse. He gathered up an old tartan blanket and a beaker of juice for her. When he came back on deck, Sylvie was nowhere to be seen.

"Sylvie?" he called out.

Where's she gone to now? Hang on, what's that?

Across the wall of the fishing harbour in the bigger bay, something moving caught his eye. He snatched up the telescope from the counter in the wheelhouse and, running to the bow, put it to his eye.

"Oh no! They're back!" he yelled.

Even though the sun was burning down, Toby felt a cold wave of sheer terror wash over him. It seemed to stop his heart beating, and paralyse him with fear.

Think! What to do? Must get Sylvie! Where is she? Where's Dad? What should I do first? Look for them?

He took a deep breath and then swung into action, racing to the top of the ladder and scanning the long quayside for his father and Sylvie. He saw his dad first, coming out of a semi-derelict shed carrying two heavy-looking jerrycans. Then he saw Sylvie who was stumbling along the quay, picking up small pebbles from the ground and stuffing them into her pyjama pockets.

Toby waved frantically. He didn't dare shout. The pirates' inflatable dinghy was some way away but he couldn't take a chance. He bobbed down behind a large buoy that sat crookedly on the concrete, and then signalled to his dad.

Luckily, just at the right moment, his dad looked up and saw him. Toby gesticulated towards the harbour. His dad understood immediately and dropped to his knees. He started to whistle quietly. It was the whistle he always used to get their attention when they were playing outside. It was only four notes but whistled in a way that they knew it was him.

Sylvie lifted her head from gazing at the ground. She smiled and tried to run towards him but fell to the ground. Toby watched in terror as his dad crawled along the gritty floor, grabbed her and pulled her and the jerrycans back inside the shed. The door closed.

Now he must act. He unwound the rope from the bollard that held the boat to the quay. Judging by the speed they were going, the pirates would arrive in a few minutes. Had he time to hide the *Lucky Lady*? He knew he had to try. The freshly painted *Lady* stuck out from the rest of the boats, like a rose in a garden of weeds. If the pirates saw her they would know that someone must be nearby. Toby couldn't let that happen.

7. A Good Game

Toby threw himself down the ladder and leapt on to the deck. He dashed into the wheelhouse and grabbed at the ignition key on the control panel. The engine turned over the first time and he gently eased the throttle forward.

Where? Where can I hide her? Toby thought desperately. *Ah!*

He had spotted two big old-fashioned fishing boats right in front of him, their hulls encrusted with barnacles and rust. They towered over the *Lucky Lady* but between them was a space where a small boat could nestle and be completely hidden from the harbour side and the quayside. The only problem was that if they moved, the small *Lucky Lady* would be crushed between them. It would be like a walnut in the grip of a nutcracker. Once mangled, *Lady* would sink like a stone into the putrid waters of the harbour.

We'll have to give it a go, I'm afraid, Lady.

Toby eased the throttle back so that the small boat crept forward into the gap. Her wireless antennae sticking up above the wheelhouse snagged on the heavy metal chains that hung from one of the fishing boats across to the other. Toby heard the antennae snap and break as *Lady* passed under the chains. The antennae were of no use anyway. There had been no radio stations for years.

Toby turned the engine off and ran to the stern to drop the anchor. He prayed that it wouldn't get caught up in the debris that must be littering the floor of the harbour. But he had no choice. He couldn't take the chance of the *Lady* drifting out into the harbour and being seen. Once she was secured, he ran to the bow and dragged an old grey tarpaulin out of the storage box. He draped it over the stern and the deckhouse, climbing up on to the roof. The canvas sheet was huge, smelly and heavy, and it took Toby all his strength to pull it up and over the roof.

Quick! Quick! Must get this on quickly!

He tugged and yanked it into place. It seemed to take him ages. But by the time he had finished it covered most of the back of the boat. If the pirates did get a view of the *Lucky Lady*, she would look like all the other old heaps sat sadly rusting away in the harbour.

Toby resisted the temptation to go and take a look to see where the pirates were. That would be stupid. They might be right behind him. He snuck under the tarpaulin and lay there, listening to the *thump, thump, thump* of his heart.

Before too long he heard the distant drone of an outboard motor. It got louder and louder. The pirates were coming into the smaller harbour at speed. He could make out the same deep male voices shouting out. They sounded in a good mood. There were screams and shrieks of laughter as the engine noise got nearer. It sounded to Toby like they were racing the boat towards something solid and then swerving around in a handbrake turn at the last second. As the boat swerved, great howls of laughter and whooping rent the air.

They're playing chicken! How long are they going to keep this up? wondered Toby. The heat under the tarpaulin was beginning to build up, stifling him. Sweat trickled down the back of his neck and into the hollow at the base of his throat. His mouth felt dry and cracked.

As the pirates continued with their game, the wash from their boat got bigger and bigger. The waves spread across the harbour, rocking the jumble of boats tangled there. Toby could feel the swell going up and down, up and down underneath him. The ups got higher and the downs got deeper, as the water slapped up the walls of the quay and bounced back against the boats. The pirates loved it. They were having a ball.

Toby lay listening to them having fun but then he heard something else — the heavy groaning and creaking of the rusty boats on either side of him. As the waves increased, the bigger boats started to move with them. He could now feel the boat on the right of him butting up against the *Lucky Lady*, nudging her over to the left where she scraped against the other fishing boat, which had also begun to roll and pitch, bouncing to the right and glancing into *Lady*. Toby felt a grinding bump as *Lady* lurched back to the right, thudding up against the first boat.

Poor Lady! She won't be able to withstand much of this, he thought desperately.

Toby wondered if he should get her out now while he could. He would have to back *Lady* out of the gap between the two boats. But the chances of not being seen seemed slim, as the pirates zoomed around the harbour. His cover would be blown. He tried to think what his dad would do.

He would stay put, and wait it out. "When in doubt do nothing," was what he said once before. Maybe that applies to this situation. I must keep my nerve. Stay here and hope they go away soon. With any luck they might have that attention deficit disorder thing that Robbie Gant at school had. He couldn't stay interested in anything for very long.

But just then Toby heard the engine noise slowing but getting louder: the pirates were coming nearer. Could they have seen the *Lucky Lady?*

"Oi, Jim! That boat tucked in there — look familiar to you? It's the same make and model as the boat from yesterday."

Toby struggled to keep the panic from rising in his throat.

"Nah, can't be. We'd have passed them if they'd come this way. Looks clean compared with most of these rusty heaps though. See if there's anything worth having on board then we'll scarper …"

Toby froze. *Stay calm, stay calm.* He crept as far into the shadows as he could and curled into a tight ball. He couldn't bear to think what the pirates would do to him if they caught him.

He soon heard someone scrabbling aboard the *Lucky Lady*, then he felt the thud of heavy footsteps on the deck.

"Hurry up, Jim — the Captain's going to flail us alive if we don't get back soon!" Toby heard the rest of the crew guffaw loudly.

"Yeah! Come on, Jim!" someone shouted. "Get moving! Don't want the Captian to get mad now, do we?"

Toby sensed the man hesitate as he approached the tarpaulin. Suddenly the tarpaulin was lifted and Toby was blinking into bright sunlight. As his eyes adjusted he realised that he was looking straight into the eyes of a pirate.

"Please don't tell them I'm here," whispered Toby frantically. "Please ..."

He stared, terrified, into the dark face of a man whose wild hair lay matted around his shoulders, and his thick black beard hung heavy with grease. The man's piercing blue eyes stared back at the thin exhausted-looking boy, lying huddled in a corner of the tarpaulin. For one moment Toby thought the man was going to call out to his pirate mates, but then the man put his finger to his lips to hush Toby.

"Quiet, lad," he whispered. "I've nae seen you."

"Oh, thank you, thank you so much ..." Toby whispered tearfully back.

"Aye, well, I had a lad of my own once ..." the pirate whispered back. "Now, stay clear of this lot. Get as far from here as you can. They're trouble!"

And with that, he dropped the tarpaulin back down. "Just a load of old junk!" he shouted across to the waiting pirates. "Enough of these games. Let's head back to the ship, quick!"

Toby, his heart still racing, lay listening to the retreating footsteps as the pirate returned to the dinghy.

In a few minutes, the waves in the harbour steadied and dropped to a gentle bobbing. The pirates had gone back to their warship. The boats stopped their ghastly groaning and quiet fell again in the harbour.

Toby heaved himself up on to shaky legs that tingled with pins and needles. He knew he must find the others and get away from the harbour. He stumbled to the back of the boat and tugged at the anchor. It was stuck; it was really stuck, embedded in something on the seabed. He pulled and pulled with all his strength, but it wouldn't budge. There was only one thing for it: he had to cut the rope. It would mean the loss of the anchor, but he needed to find his dad and Sylvie quickly. He had a horrible feeling that the pirates hadn't had all their fun from Peterhead harbour. He was sure that they would come back, and soon.

Once he had cut the rope, he swung the boat back to the quay to where it had been before. Sprinting up the ladder and along the quay to the shed, he knocked tentatively on the door.

"Dad? You still there?" he cried. "You can come out now, they've gone."

There was no answer.

Toby carefully opened the door. Inside the shed it was dark and cobwebby. He bent down to pick something off the floor. It was a teddy. It was Sylvie's teddy, but where was Sylvie?

He crept further into the shed. It had been a fisherman's

bothy where he would have stored ropes, provisions, nets and nylon for mending them. There was a stack of dusty lobster creels in one corner, and in another corner a tarpaulin lay draped over something lumpy.

Toby flinched with fright.

"Dad?" he gasped. Toby edged forward slowly, and nudged the lump with his foot. Nothing.

Toby grabbed the corner of the tarpaulin and yanked it off whatever lay underneath.

"Oh, what a fright you gave me!" he cried. There, cuddled up in the corner on a pile of old sheeting, were his dad and Sylvie. They were both fast asleep.

"Dad! Come on! We must go!" Toby was enjoying being the one in charge now.

"Huh?" groaned his dad sleepily. Toby shook him vigorously.

"Dad, come on, wake up. They might be back. One of them saw me — but he let me go … and then I thought I was going to get crushed! Come on, quick, and I'll tell you all about it!"

"I must've been tired. I can't believe I slept through all of that … They saw you?" said his father, shaking his head in disbelief as he bent down to scoop up the sleepy Sylvie.

"Wait a minute," cried Toby. "I'm going to bring a couple of these with me. They might come in handy." He grabbed a couple of the dusty lobster pots from the pile in the corner and, struggling out the door, made his way back to the boat.

The three of them were soon back on board the *Lucky Lady*. Toby struggled to stow the heavy jerrycans on deck, whilst his father took Sylvie back to her bed. After lashing two of the cans safely together and emptying the other one into the fuel tank, Toby went to find his dad. He was washing all the dust and grit from Sylvie's face and hands.

"We'd better get going, Dad," said Toby breathlessly. "Are we going home now?"

"Yep, we've just enough fuel and supplies to get back now," he replied. "You finish off here. I'll get us out of here." He pecked Sylvie on the cheek, and dashed from the cabin.

"Are we going home now?" asked Sylvie, snuggling down her bed.

"Yeah, won't that be great?" replied Toby. "I'm worn out by all this excitement. I want to sleep for a week in my comfy bed."

"What were those men doing?" she asked.

"Oh, just having a bit of fun, I suppose," said Toby. "Come on, let's get you out of those pyjamas. They're filthy."

Once he'd made sure Sylvie was clean and comfortable, Toby went up on deck to talk to his father. His dad looked hollow eyed and sunken faced. The tension of the last few days had taken its toll on him, and he looked a lot older than his forty years.

"Can we risk going home?" Toby asked him.

"We'll have to," he replied. "We can't keep this up. It's too stressful for all of us, especially Sylvie. We need to get home and get some proper sleep and food. Anyway, the chickens will starve if we don't go back soon."

"D'you think the pirates will come looking for us?"

"I'm not sure," said his dad. "They may be more interested in what they can scavenge from Peterhead now. It looked like there was still a lot of stuff lying around. There may be some fuel left in the big tanks up by the breakwaters. And there's probably some fuel to be siphoned out of all those little boats in the fishing harbour. Depends how desperate they are."

"We're not far from home here, are we?" asked Toby.

"No, not far at all."

"Dad," blurted Toby, "do you think Sylvie has red fever?" He just had to ask; he'd been worrying about it so long.

"Let's not talk about that now, son," sighed his dad. "Let's get her home. We'll be there soon, don't worry. Now, tell me about what happened in the harbour. A pirate saw you — and he didn't let on?"

"Yes, it was weird. He could have told the others I was hiding under the tarpaulin but instead he told me he'd had a son once and then warned me to get away from the others — said they were trouble. Why do you think that was?"

"It just shows that people get involved in some terrible things when they're desperate to survive. Sounds like he's not a bad man — he's obviously lost his son."

Toby told his dad about how scared he'd been when the boats started bobbing around and he thought the *Lucky Lady* was going to be crushed.

"You did well to get us out of that scrape, son, but we still need to be on our guard. You'd better go and keep watch."

Toby went out into the afternoon sunshine and scanned the horizon. He watched the waves foaming beside them as the *Lucky Lady* cruised across the harbour and out into the ocean. It was a beautiful sunny day. It was hard to believe that the world could be such a dangerous place on a lovely day like this. The boat swung right under the headland where the tall white prison building stood. There was no sign of the dogs. The boat struck out towards the cliffs at Buchan Ness. It felt good to have the sun on his face and the wind rippling his hair. He really must get his dad to cut it; the long straggles had reached his shoulders. He went inside to get his woolly hat; even on a sunny day the sea breeze made his ears tingle with cold.

Back on deck, Toby watched his dad expertly handling the boat as it scudded across the sea.

"Dad?" Toby asked. "What happened to all the prisoners in the jails when the sickness came?"

"I'm not sure," answered his dad. "I suppose they died like so many did. Any infection would spread like wildfire in a place like that. I heard various stories at the time. Horrible stories, I'd rather not repeat."

"D'you think a lot of them escaped?"

"I don't think so, Tobes. The government put the country into a state of emergency quite quickly, and the army took over the running of a lot of these places."

"So what happened to the army?" said Toby.

"It eventually fell apart too," replied his dad.

"Was there an army base near here?"

"I think the nearest one was at Fort George, near Inverness. But I heard that it had fallen into disorder, everyone deserted. The soldiers wanted to get back to their families and take care of them, I suppose."

Toby realised that this was the first conversation they had really had about the epidemic. Maybe his dad had thought him too young at the time to discuss it. Toby really didn't remember much about what had happened at the start. The first sign that his world was changing was when their school closed, and then his dad stopped going to work. Not long after that they left the cottage and moved into the lighthouse.

"Why didn't we die?" asked Toby.

His dad turned to look at him. "I really don't know, Toby. I can only think that in every population there are some people who have a natural immunity to certain things. Not everyone died."

"No, we're still here, aren't we?" said Toby. His dad smiled faintly.

"Yes, we're still here," he said. "Even if it is just by the skin of our teeth."

Toby smiled sadly at his dad.

But at least we're still here.

8. A Boy and his Dog

The *Lucky Lady* was making good progress. They were soon motoring past the towering arches at the Bullers of Buchan. They could hear the clamour of thousands of seabirds long before they caught sight of them wheeling and diving, fighting over nesting ledges and spitting at their neighbours. Toby's dad pointed out the cave where they'd so nearly been discovered by the pirates. That seemed such a long time ago. So much had happened.

They cruised on, past the gothic-looking remains of Slains Castle, perched high above the sea. Toby remembered his mum telling him a tale about a long-ago queen at Slains, who had been hung out over the cliff in a wire basket as punishment for her husband's disloyalty to his clan.

How could someone do that to someone else? he thought. But he knew now that people were capable of doing terrible things to one another.

As the boat rounded the peninsula at Port Errol, they saw the long white stretch of sand at Cruden Bay. This had been a favourite place to go. Long summer days had been spent sitting on the beach with buckets and spades, digging holes in the wet sand.

"See who's the first to get to Australia," his mum had joked, as he and his dad competed to dig the biggest hole. They always took a kite and ran across the sand, laughing and shouting as it dipped and dived. It would take off on a gust of wind, only to land with a plop at the sea's edge. To get back to the car they had to cross a bridge over the estuary river. Monty had hated that bridge as there were gaps between the planks and he was scared of putting his paws down the holes. Once back in the car park, they all had an ice-cream cone with a chocolate flake, even Monty.

Toby picked up the telescope and went out to the prow. He wanted to see if he could spot the place on the dunes where he had jumped down to the beach in two great big leaps, the spiky marron grass cutting into his toes.

"Dad!" he shouted. "There's someone on the beach!"

He raised the glass to his eye again. Yes, there they were! Someone was running across the sand towards the bridge. He couldn't make out whether it was a boy or a girl. And there running alongside them was a dog. It was a big dog, a big white dog.

"DAD! Look!"

"Where?" his dad yelled from the wheelhouse.

"Turn round! Turn the boat round, now!" screamed Toby. "Somebody's chasing them!"

He could now see with his naked eye that it was a boy running across the sand as fast as he could, with the dog alongside him. As he watched, a man came running out of the sand dunes, waving something in his hand. He looked scary. His mouth was opening and closing as if he were shouting something. The boy stumbled as he turned to look over his shoulder at the man. The dog bounced beside him, pushing at him with its nose.

"Hurry! He's in trouble!"

The *Lucky Lady* turned around and swung in towards the beach.

"I can't take her in much further," cried his dad. "She'll run aground on a sand bank and then we'll be stuck."

Toby could now see that the man was brandishing a baseball bat and he looked like he intended to use it.

"We're over here! Swim! It's your only chance!" he yelled at the top of his voice. "Dad, use the foghorn, go on!"

"I can't. The pirates may be close," shouted his dad.

Toby ran to the back of the boat, slipped the towing rope from its cleat and jumped into the rubber dinghy. He grabbed the oars from the floor, stuck them into the rowlocks and started rowing with all his strength.

"Toby!" yelled his dad. "Watch out for the cross-current — where the estuary comes into the sea."

Toby cast a glance over his shoulder to see where the boy was. He was still running down the beach towards the estuary bridge.

"No! Don't go that way! Get into the water and swim!" he screamed, but the boy was still too far away to hear him.

The man had slowed down. He looked like he was struggling through the heavy sand at the foot of the dunes. The boy was now running up the side of the dunes, away from the beach and towards the bridge.

Please, please, boy, get into the water and swim. I haven't got the strength to fight the current and row up river. If only I had time to start the outboard motor.

But he didn't have time and he wasn't sure if there was any diesel in it anyway. The boy was now sprinting over the wooden bridge. It must have become dilapidated since Toby and his family had enjoyed picnics there, as he saw the boy and the dog leaping from plank to plank across huge gaps.

His dog's braver than Monty, thought Toby.

Suddenly a strong pull on the dinghy wrenched it sideways, almost pulling the oars from Toby's hands. He had entered the cross-current where the river entering the sea met the tide. The small craft bounced crazily and then swirled around to face out to sea.

Toby pulled on the oars with all the muscle he could muster. He wasn't as strong as he used to be. He managed to pull the dinghy round so that its nose was facing directly up the river mouth. He could see his dad on board the *Lucky Lady*, waving frantically at him to head to the other side of the estuary.

Where does he want me to go? he thought desperately. *And where has the boy gone?*

The man had reached the foot of the bridge and was limping up the steps. He had seen Toby and stopped to wave his baseball bat angrily at him, shouting something that Toby couldn't hear.

A final mighty pull on the oars and the dinghy was out of the cross-current and heading round the edge of a promontory on which there was a cluster of fishing bothies. Toby could see the stands where the fishermen had thrown their nets to dry and mend. A few pieces of rotted net still stuck to the metal uprights. He caught a glimpse of the boy and the dog, running along a track which led to the other side of the shacks.

Faster, come on! Row faster!

Toby looked up to see that the *Lucky Lady* was sitting just outside the small harbour. His dad was still waving for him to go into the harbour.

Why? Couldn't he take the Lucky Lady *into the harbour?*

The boy and dog suddenly appeared on the harbour wall. The boy was wild eyed and gasping for breath. He looked petrified.

Woof! The dog barked at Toby as he bashed the dinghy against the wall of the harbour. The boy pointed to some harbour steps that led into the water, ten metres from him. Toby manoeuvred the dinghy as quickly as he could. He could see the boy nervously watching the track for the man to appear. The dog barked and jumped up and down, its tail wagging furiously, as if it was all a good game.

"Get in! Quick!" shouted Toby, leaning over and hanging on to the side of the harbour wall with his bare hands. There was no time to tie up. The boy half leapt, half crawled over the side of the dinghy.

"Belle! Come!" the boy commanded the dog, which jumped cleanly into the middle of the dinghy. The impact of its weight made the dinghy bounce away from the harbour wall. As he tried to hang on, Toby felt his fingernails scratching down the gritty granite surface, setting his teeth on edge. He pulled himself upright and grasped the oars.

"Let's go!" he said, pushing an oar against the wall and bracing his back to row.

"He's coming!" shouted the boy, holding tight on to the dog. "Hurry!"

Well, I'm not going to hang around, am I now? thought Toby.

The dinghy pulled slowly away from the steps. The addition of the two passengers made it much harder to row, and Toby was struggling to make any progress.

"Let me help," suggested the boy, squirming over so that he sat next to Toby on the wooden bench. Before Toby could argue, he had taken an oar and was pulling it hard into the water. The dinghy swirled in the opposite direction.

"Whoa! We need to do this together. Now, one — two — three … PULL!" cried Toby.

"Stop! Stop right there! That dog's …" the man shouted as he ran towards the harbour, but Toby couldn't hear what he said next, as they were now making good headway out of the mouth of the harbour. He could hear the puttering of *Lady*'s engine nearby.

"Toby! Over here!" shouted his dad.

Toby felt the rise and fall of the waves increase as the wash from *Lady* hit the dinghy. They drew nearer until he felt the bump of the dinghy's rubber side bash against the hard wood of the bigger boat.

The boy had already leapt up and was throwing a rope over the side for Toby's dad to catch. The *Lucky Lady* was bouncing and dancing on the waves but the boy had no problem shimmying up its side and on to the deck. The dog barked at him as he left.

"It's OK, boys. The guy's given up. Relax, he's not chasing you any more," Toby's dad reassured them.

"Phew! That was close! What on earth was that about?" yelled Toby, catching his breath, still sitting in the dinghy.

"He wanted to kill Belle," the boy stated.

"Kill her? Why? Because she's a dog?" asked Toby's dad. The boy nodded, looking at the dog. She gave a big sloppy dog grin.

"I can't see this one hurting anyone," said Toby. "Let's get her on board, then. I'll heave from behind if you catch the front end," he said to the boy. "It's a bit far to jump."

"Hold on a mo!" said his dad. "I'm not sure I want that dog on board this boat."

"What?" cried Toby. "What are you on about, Dad? It's this boy's dog. The man was going to kill it so we rescued them. Both of them."

"We don't know why he wanted to kill it, do we? There might have been a very good reason," said his father.

"Do we have to discuss this now?" asked Toby. "For

all we know he's gone to get a shotgun and he's coming back to blast us all out of the water!"

"OK! OK!" yelled his dad. "Let's get it on board and go. But I hold you responsible for its behaviour, young man," he said to the boy.

The boy nodded once more. "Thank you," he said. "Come, Belle!" he shouted to the dog, which backed up a couple of steps in the dinghy, then sprang into the air as if it was a cat. It landed half on the deck and half on the boy, who gave it a big hug.

"I knew you could do it! Clever dog!" he gasped.

"Great," moaned Toby. "Now can someone give me a hand?" The boy leant over and offered him his hand. "Thanks," said Toby, springing up beside him.

He untied the dinghy and dragged it round the side of the boat, then retied it to the stern. The boy and the dog nestled themselves in the prow of the boat, seemingly unfazed at what had just happened.

Toby's nerves were shattered and he started to shake. He was shocked at the ferocity of the man chasing the boy and at his dad's apparent lack of concern for his safety.

"Dad?" he asked. "Why didn't you bring *Lady* into the harbour? I nearly didn't make it."

"I couldn't take *Lady* into the harbour. I couldn't risk that man getting on board."

Toby stared angrily at his dad, even though he knew that he was right.

"Toby, I wouldn't have let him hurt you," his dad insisted. "I didn't know how deep the harbour was either. I didn't want to go aground."

"So you left it to me to rescue the boy ... Cheers, Dad." Toby felt a hot and furious anger towards him. His father had been willing to gamble on his son's life to protect his own and Sylvie's.

"Here, you're in shock," said his dad, offering Toby a large fleecy jacket. "Go to the cabin and keep warm. I'll keep an eye on these two." He motioned to the boy and dog, who were sitting in front of the wheelhouse. "We'll be home soon."

Toby shrugged off the jacket and stormed out.

9. Jamie McTavish

Sylvie's bed was covered in Barbie dolls and scraps of fabric. She usually loved to make dresses and outfits for them, but she'd got them out and felt too poorly to make anything new.

Toby put his hand to her forehead. She was burning up, and her rash still looked red and angry.

"How are you feeling, Sylve?" asked Toby.

"Not very well," she snuffled, trying to sit up.

"Shh, just you rest now," said Toby.

"I had a really long sleep," said Sylvie. "I dreamt I heard a dog barking. Then I heard its claws *scrat, scrat, scratting* on the deck. It was horrible, Tobes."

"Ah, well, Sylvie, whilst you've been asleep, something has happened. We've a boy come aboard."

"A real boy?" she gasped.

"Yep, a real boy and he has a real dog with him."

"A dog?" she croaked, dropping all her Barbies on the floor. "No, Toby, tell me it's not true! Tell me you're making it up, aren't you?"

"No, Sylvie," he said gently. "I'm not. But you mustn't be scared of this dog because she is just like Monty was. She's a big friendly dog. You'll see."

"A big dog?" Sylvie exclaimed. "I don't want to see a big dog. I don't like big dogs, Toby, you know I don't!" Toby could she see was getting panicky. The little colour she'd had had drained from her face and her eyes were wide with fear.

"It's OK, honest. You'll love this dog. She's like a big fluffy teddy bear. But if you don't want to meet her, that's OK too. She won't be coming in here, and we'll be home soon, and then she'll be gone."

"We'll be home soon?" she asked. "Oh, I want to be at home. I want to see my chickens again, and Henry's sick of being cooped up in his hutch. I want to feel better so we can go outside and play again. Are you going to come and play too, Toby?"

"Yes, I'll come and play. That'll be great. Now let's get all this Barbie stuff tidied up before Dad sees it. Y'know what a stickler he is for being tidy." Actually, his dad was very tolerant of Sylvie's messes; in fact, anything Sylvie did was OK with his dad.

Toby tousled the top of Sylvie's hair with his hand. He did love her. She reminded him of his mum, and though that was painful, it also felt like a bit of his mum was always with him.

Toby pulled on several thick jumpers and a pair of woolly gloves. His hand had been getting sorer but he hadn't had time to think about it. He winced as he pulled the glove over the stained and grubby hankie that was still acting as a dressing. He was so cold, even with all the layers on, but he went outside anyway. He wanted to speak to the boy.

He found the boy and his dog exactly where he'd left them. They were sitting staring out to sea at the front of the prow. He sat down beside them.

"Thanks for saving me and Belle. We wouldn't have made it without you coming along at just the right moment. I was so scared, my legs were turning to jelly," said the boy.

"So why didn't you swim for it?" Toby asked, trying hard to keep the anger out of his voice. "If you'd just got into the water and swam out a little I'd have got you much quicker. You wouldn't have had to run so …"

"I can't swim," the boy stated quietly.

"What?" Toby was shocked. He'd never heard of anyone young not being able to swim before. Yes, his gran hadn't been able to swim, and neither had old Mrs Pratt who lived in the village, but they'd been ancient.

"I'm not proud of it," said the boy. "I never learnt, that's all. Mum was always busy with her work. Too busy to take me to swimming lessons. No big deal."

"What about your dad?" asked Toby. His dad had driven him to the local town every Saturday morning for years, and sat and read the paper while Toby had struggled up and down the pool. Finally he'd become a confident swimmer and then his dad had been happy to take him sailing with him. But Toby hadn't wanted to go.

"Never had a dad," said the boy.

Lucky you, thought Toby, but then he felt a pang of disloyalty. He didn't really think that about his dad, at least not all the time.

"Oh, I'm sorry," he said instead.

"It's OK. You can't miss what you never had," replied the boy in a matter-of-fact manner.

"So, anyway, what's your name? Mine's Toby, Toby Tennant."

"Oh, yeah, sorry." The boy put his hand out for Toby to shake. "Mine's Jamie, Jamie McTavish." Jamie took hold of Toby's hand and shook it in a serious, adult sort of way.

"Ah!" yelped Toby. "That hurts."

"I'm sorry," said Jamie. "Let me have a look. I'm good

with wounds and things. Went on a first-aid course with the Cub Scouts once."

"You're not old enough to have been a Scout!" declared Toby.

"I'm thirteen," declared Jamie.

"Really? You don't look it; sorry but it's true," said Toby.

Jamie took Toby's hand and started to unpeel the hankie, but blood and dirt had glued it to the skin. Jamie left him for a while and then came back with a bowl of bottled water.

"What are you going to do with that?" asked Toby.

"I'm not going to be able to get this yucky hankie off without soaking your hand first," said Jamie.

"OK, OK. Whatever." Toby put his hand into the ice-cold water. "Ah!" he yelled. "That's cold!"

"Hold still," commanded Jamie.

With his hand soaking in the water, Toby had time to look at the boy while they sat chatting. He was very fair, with silvery-blond hair that fell in curls to his shoulders.

Bet he got a hard time for that when he was at school, thought Toby.

The boy's skin was pale, milky white. It wasn't white like Sylvie's, whose skin had a strange white-grey pallor. His had a transparency to it so that the blue of his veins could be seen at his temples and wrists. When Jamie looked at him, Toby could see that his eyes were a brilliant, piercing blue, almost like the sea itself — only not the North Sea, more like the Mediterranean.

The dog sat quietly at Jamie's side, watching out to sea with pricked ears.

"She's very bonny," said Toby. "What sort of dog is she?"

"She's a Pyrenean mountain dog. That's not a sort, that's a breed," replied Jamie.

"I didn't think there were any pure-bred dogs left. I thought there were only mongrels these days."

"My mum bred her herself. She'd always had mountain dogs. She bred her mother and her mother's mother. Belle is the last one."

"Why did that man want to kill her?"

"Er, well, she bit him," said Jamie.

"She *bit* him? Oh, great!" exclaimed Toby, pushing himself away from the dog. "Was there a reason?"

"Yes, the man was going to hit me. He raised his hand to strike me and Belle went for him."

"Why would he want to hit you?"

"I had something he wanted and I wouldn't give it to him," replied Jamie.

"Why didn't you just give him what he wanted? It can't have been that important."

"You're wrong. It was. It was my mum's locket with her picture in, and a lock of her hair."

"Oh, yeah, I can see that would be important to you," said Toby, assuming that, like him, Jamie had lost his mum. "Look, don't tell my dad about Belle biting that man. He'll have her overboard like a shot. He's not keen on dogs any more. You can understand that, eh?"

Jamie nodded, and put his arm round Belle. "Yeah, I can understand that. Belle's different, but I can't expect other folk to realise that, especially when she goes around biting people. But she was defending me, honest."

"Well, can you get on with sorting out this hand before it drops off with the cold?" suggested Toby, pulling a soggy mess of hanky and hand out of the bowl.

Jamie unwrapped it slowly, taking care not to pull the skin underneath off with the hankie.

"Doesn't smell too good, does it?" remarked Toby, who was trying to be brave. The hand was inflamed and a violent reddy-purple colour. Jamie seemed intensely interested in state of Toby's knuckles.

"I wanted to be a doctor," he explained. "My mum's a doctor and a psychologist; I get it from her."

Funny, I thought he said his mum IS a doctor. That sounds like she's still alive, thought Toby.

"I'm going to need a first-aid kit. Have you got one?" enquired Jamie.

"Nothing much left in it, I'm afraid. Some sticking

plasters and bandages; that's about it, I think. We've been looking everywhere for stuff for Sylvie. She's my little sister. She's sick but we don't know what with … Oh, don't worry, it's not red fever," Toby lied. Maybe this boy could help his little sister. "No, it's since Mum died, it's like Sylvie's pining away. Come and meet her. I think there's a first-aid tin in the cabin."

When the two boys went into the cabin, Sylvie was looking a bit better. She was sitting up in bed combing Henry's hair.

"Oh no!" she squeaked. "Don't bring the dog in! It'll eat Henry!"

"It's OK, it's OK, Sylvie. Belle's tied up outside," Toby assured her. "This is Jamie, the boy I was telling you about."

Sylvie suddenly burrowed down into her bedclothes. "Hello," said a much muffled-sounding Sylvie.

Toby laughed. He'd never seen her act shy before.

Sylvie was so curious to know what he was laughing about that she soon popped up, clutching Henry in her hand. The rabbit had a surprised look on its face.

Toby laughed louder. It was a relief to laugh after all the tension of the day. Toby sensed his anger against his dad and Jamie subsiding.

Jamie was sitting quietly on the other bunk. He had an aura of peace and calm about him. Sylvie, her shyness forgotten, appeared to be mesmerised by him and sat staring at the pale boy.

Jamie cleaned and dressed Toby's hand, carefully cutting the dead skin away with a pair of Sylvie's craft scissors that he'd sterilised in hot water. Toby bit his lip and tried to think of ice cream with chocolate flakes to take his mind off the pain. Sylvie couldn't watch and hid under her bedclothes.

"Is it safe to come out yet?" came a dim voice from under the duvet.

"Yep, I'm done," said Jamie, tidying away the tissues and iodine that he'd used. "You need to keep that clean, Toby. There's still infection in the wound."

Toby mopped his face with a tissue. He didn't feel great. He felt like he was burning up. Globules of sweat glistened on his forehead, and the sick feeling had returned. He threw off the heavy layers of clothing he'd been wearing.

"It's hot in here!" he gasped hoarsely. His throat was parched and he was *so* thirsty. "I need a drink of water."

He stumbled out of the cabin towards the stack of bottled water, but he didn't make it. He collapsed with a thud on to the floor.

10. A Crazy World

When Toby woke up he found himself in his own room in the lighthouse in Collieston.

I'm dreaming, he thought. *Must be. The last thing I remember was, er ... was chatting to Sylvie and ... Jamie?*

He sat up in his bed then winced. There was a large white pad on his right hand. He remembered now. Jamie had put a fresh bandage on his hand, and then?

"Hi! How are you feeling?" asked his dad, rubbing his eyes. "I've been sleeping right here, to keep an eye on you." His dad unfurled himself from the old armchair by the window.

"How long have I been here?" croaked Toby. His throat still felt sore and dry.

"A couple of days. We got back not long after you

passed out. You've had a fever," said his dad.

"I feel … I'm not sure yet. I feel a bit funny. Sort of light-headed. Is this what a hangover feels like?" asked Toby, propping himself up on his pillows.

"I don't know, haven't had one since I was a student. You gave us a nasty fright. Jamie thinks you had blood poisoning from that wound on your hand. When you started to burn up, I didn't know what to do. In the old days, the doctors would have pumped you full of antibiotics. But we've not had much luck finding any of those, have we?"

"So what happened?" asked Toby. He was puzzled. How come, according to his dad, he was dying one moment, and the next … well, here he was.

"It was Jamie. I'm not quite sure what he did. He made a poultice for your hand, out of seaweed or something. Then he made this weird-smelling drink out of some dried fungi he had in his pocket. Next thing I know, your temperature has dropped and you're sleeping like a baby."

"Are you sure? That sounds so weird," said Toby.

"Yeah, I'm sure. But why didn't you tell me you'd hurt yourself? I could have dressed that for you before it went septic!" His dad was trying hard not to sound cross with him, but Toby could see that he hadn't needed anything else to worry about. He looked exhausted.

"There wasn't time, Dad. Everything happened so quickly," said Toby. "I didn't realise how bad it had got."

"OK, I know, Tobes. It was a pretty rough mission, wasn't it? Eh? Well, we're home again now. Trouble is, we're no better off then we were. We didn't find any medicines. In fact, we're worse off. We've got another mouth to feed now."

"Two. We've got two extra mouths to feed now," Toby corrected him.

"Huh, if Jamie thinks I'm going to feed that enormous dog, he's mistaken. He'll have to scavenge for it, on his own."

"Be fair, Dad. He can't do that. From what you're saying, he saved my life. And maybe he'll be able to help Sylvie. We'll give him our scraps to feed Belle."

"What do you mean scraps?" snapped his dad. "We've never any leftovers. Anything we don't eat goes into the soup pot or the chickens' feed."

Toby sighed; he didn't feel up to arguing with his dad. His body ached and his hand throbbed. He wanted to sleep and wake up to find all the problems and worries of his world had been solved by someone, as if by magic.

I can't think right now, I'm so tired, and I just want to go to sleep. I'll think about this later.

Toby yawned, turned over and was asleep in seconds.

His next visitor was Jamie, who crept into his bedroom and peered quizzically at him.

"Hi, Toby, how's it going?" said Jamie quietly.

"Oh, oh," groaned Toby. "My head hurts, in fact everything hurts."

"Here, drink this." Jamie held out a chipped mug full of a pink gooey substance that Toby wouldn't have described as a drink.

"What's that?" asked Toby, pulling himself carefully into a sitting position.

"Call it a health drink," said Jamie. "I've been out gathering berries and stuff. Did you know you've got a really good harvest of blaeberries on the cliffs round the corner?"

"Blaeberries?" said Toby. "On the cliffs? What were you doing on the cliffs? Don't you know it's dangerous? What if the dogs had seen you?"

"I had Belle with me. She stands guard whilst I forage for anything that might be of use. You'd be amazed at what's out there."

"Yeah? I'd be amazed if there was anything nice out there," said Toby ruefully, "especially anything worth the risk of being attacked by the dogs!"

"Do you have much trouble from the local dogs?" asked Jamie.

"Yeah, some," replied Toby gruffly. "That's why

Dad put those huge gates up outside the compound."

"This is a great place," said Jamie, wandering around Toby's bedroom. "Must be really cool to live in a lighthouse."

"It was a right dump when we moved in, but Dad's done a lot to it," said Toby. He swung his legs out of the bed. "Hey, I'm feeling a bit better now. My head's stopped throbbing. Pass me my clothes and I'll get up and give you a tour."

Toby started his tour of the lighthouse at the very top. The boys climbed up the wooden ladder into the sun-filled lamp room.

"This is the best room in the house," said Toby. He loved it up here. He felt like he was in a balloon, floating over the blue sea, with the gulls calling to him as they flew alongside. There were huge windows all the way round through which the sunlight danced, bouncing off the massive silvery lenses in the centre.

"Wow!" exclaimed Jamie. "What a view!" The expanse of sparkling blue sea stretched out below them for miles and miles and miles.

"Dad's got the light working again," said Toby, proudly, pointing to the eight highly-polished lenses in the middle of the room. They sat on a circular frame under which there was a whole arrangement of brass cogs and wheels.

"See," he pointed to the lamp in the centre, "that's the source of light. These lenses magnify it and send the light out for miles. This mechanism under here rotates the lenses on this frame so that a different pattern of light is sent out from each lighthouse. Clever, eh?"

"Why's that then?" asked Jamie.

"So the sailors knew where they were from the different patterns from different lighthouses, you muppet," laughed Toby. Sometimes, for someone who appeared to be so clever, Jamie was incredibly stupid.

"Dad and I take it in turns to keep watch up here. See, we've got a telescope too." Toby pointed to the tripod and large telescope which sat in the narrow galley that went round the room between the lenses and the windows. "Have a look."

Jamie pulled the telescope eyepiece towards him.

"Can you see Aberdeen from here?" he asked.

"Yeah, on a clear day. You can see the tower blocks down by the beach at the Bridge of Don," replied Toby.

"How far is it from here, by boat I mean?" Jamie asked.

"I'm not sure really. Can't be that far. It used to take us less than an hour by car to get to Aberdeen, and if anything it's nearer by boat. You can travel as the crow flies, straight there."

"Really?" Jamie swung the telescope round to face

southwards. "Yes, you're right, I can see the tower blocks poking up."

"D'you know Aberdeen at all?" asked Toby.

"My mum and I lived there. Then when Cerberus took over, we moved out to Newburgh, where the experimental station is."

"Whoa, whoa! Hang on a minute. Who's Cerberus? And what do you mean took over?" exclaimed Toby. Jamie kept his eye fixed on the distant spot that was Aberdeen.

"Cerberus is the leader of the dogs in Aberdeen. He controls the whole city now."

"What? You're trying to tell me that this Cerberus is in charge of all the dogs in Aberdeen? That's barmy! How can a dog do that? And who called it Cerberus anyway? You'll be telling me next that dogs have learnt to talk!"

"My mum called him Cerberus, after the three-headed hound that guards the gates of hell. And no, they haven't learnt to talk, but they have learnt how to work together to survive. They already knew how to communicate, just not in words," explained Jamie.

"How come you know all this?"

"My mum, I told you, she's a scientist. She used to work on human behaviour at the Rowett Research Institute, but since the dogs went wild, she's been studying them."

"So where is she now?" Toby was intrigued. This story was getting weirder and weirder.

"Aberdeen," said Jamie quietly.

"What? You're joking? Aberdeen's been a no-go zone for over a year now. She doesn't stand a chance … she can't still be alive …" Toby suddenly realised what he was saying. "Sorry, Jamie, I didn't mean …"

"No, you're wrong. I know she's still alive. I can sense her. I'd know if anything had happened to her."

Toby felt overwhelmingly sad. He could remember how he had reacted to his mum's accident. He hadn't wanted to believe it. And afterwards, sometimes, he had sensed her, as if she had never gone away.

"Look, Jamie, I know how you're feeling right now. Believe me, I do. But you need to come to grips with the loss of …"

"She is not dead, I tell you!" Jamie screamed back at Toby.

"OK, OK, so she's not dead. Calm down. You'll upset Sylvie if she hears you shouting." Toby tried to soothe the boy who was facing him, with his blue eyes staring piercingly at him.

He looks scary when he does that!

Jamie's outburst shocked him. He hadn't seen much of Jamie since they rescued him, but he'd got the impression that he was a very quiet, almost withdrawn boy. He was obviously wrong.

"I'm sorry," said Jamie. "But she really is alive. She went to Aberdeen to study the dog packs there. I saw her a couple of months ago. She came back to the station for a few days to see if I was OK."

"What? She left you at Newburgh on your own?" said Toby incredulously, but then remembered that *his* dad had sent him alone on to an oil platform.

"I wasn't alone. I was with a girl called Maggie who used to work at the same place as my mum. But then this man came and Maggie wanted to go with him, so I had to go too. They forced me to go with them. That's how I ended up at Cruden Bay."

"So as far as you know, your mum is still in Aberdeen?" asked Toby.

"Yes, she was supposed to come back and fetch me once she'd finished her research. But she never came. So Maggie said she wasn't coming back and we had to move because the packs were getting nearer."

"What d'you mean, the packs were getting nearer?"

"It's like I told you. The dogs are getting organised. The packs are coming out of Aberdeen under Cerberus's command and taking over everything."

"This sounds *so* weird. You'd better tell my dad. Come on, let's find him."

Toby's dad was outside in the yard splitting logs for the stove. The yard was inside the lighthouse's compound, with tall walls surrounding it. They had fixed reels of barbed wire on the top of the walls to stop the dogs jumping over. Outside the compound were more gates and wire fencing to stop the dogs getting on to the promontory on which the lighthouse stood.

"Dad!" Toby called. His dad came over to the two boys. "You need to hear what Jamie has to say about the dogs," Toby told him. The three of them sat on an old bench and Jamie repeated what he had just told Toby. His dad rubbed the sweat from his brow with a grimy hand.

"I'd heard stories from folk who'd stopped in Aberdeen. It sounded pretty grim. One of them had seen a big black dog leading a pack of dogs. The guy said that the pack seemed to be patrolling the harbour, on the lookout for new ships coming in. The folk thought it was too dangerous so they didn't get off the boat."

"Patrolling? Are dogs clever enough to do that?" asked Toby.

"Yes, according to my mum, they are," said Jamie. "She said that Cerberus appeared to have organised the dogs into battalions, y'know like an army has? Each battalion was given its own area to patrol."

"What's your mum doing there?" asked Toby's dad. Toby could see that his dad was taking Jamie's story seriously.

I think the boy's mad! I mean, some cranky crackpot story of dogs acting like soldiers! How nutty does that sound?

"She's been studying the dogs for about two years now. She knows Aberdeen really well; she grew up there. Her dad, my grandpaps, was a caretaker at Marischal College. When she was a girl he showed her a set of passageways under the college. I think they were part of the ancient sewerage system running under the city. She's been using them to get about and spy on the dogs."

"That's a very risky thing to do," said Toby's dad, the concern showing in his face. "What if they smell her? Dogs have a highly sensitive sense of smell."

Jamie smiled the first smile that Toby had seen on his face. "Mum has a way of dealing with that. She found a dead badger and cooked it. Then she sprayed the juice all over herself. Dogs hate badgers and won't go anywhere near them."

"Yuck!" said Toby and his dad together.

"Yeah, right! Pretty gross, eh?" said Jamie. "Mum's great. She doesn't care as long as she gets the job done."

"D'you know why she's doing this?" asked Toby's dad.

"She thinks the dogs are evolving at an extra quick rate," replied Jamie. "Something to do with cross-infection with the red fever virus. The dogs' powers are super-evolving and they're getting cleverer and cleverer. That's her theory, anyway."

"Super-evolving?" quizzed Toby's dad. "Cross-infection with the virus? I don't know, Jamie. It all sounds a bit iffy to me."

"My mum's a scientist. She has two degrees!" Jamie stared defiantly at Toby and his dad. "Who are you to disagree with her?"

"Er, yep, I'm just a humble engineer. You're right, what would I know about dog behaviour and evolution? But are you sure your mum was … well … was thinking straight when she came up with these ideas? They do sound a bit crazy."

"Crazy?" shouted Jamie, standing up and facing them. "Hasn't the whole world gone crazy? Isn't it crazy that red fever has wiped out most of mankind?" His hands were clenched into tight fists and he looked like he was about to hit one of them. Then, before Toby or his dad could say a word, Jamie turned on his heels and stormed off.

11. Arrival of the Foot Soldiers

Later, when Toby had finished his chores, he began to feel a little queasy and light-headed again. He decided to go and lie down on his bed for a nap. As he was going up the stone steps which coiled around the inner wall of the lighthouse, he passed the door to his dad's bedroom. Here his dad slept, with a small truckle bed in the corner for Sylvie. During the day Sylvie was carried downstairs to lie on an old sofa in the kitchen so she could watch all the comings and goings of the house.

The door of the bedroom was slightly ajar. Toby could hear hushed voices coming from inside. He stood at the door listening. It was his dad talking to Jamie about Sylvie. A rush of jealousy ran through Toby. His dad never talked to him like this about Sylvie. He was explaining how Sylvie's health had been slowly getting worse and how her symptoms were so changeable. Some days she appeared to be getting better and other days she was weak and feverish with pains in all her limbs so bad that she couldn't walk. She had got weaker and weaker as her appetite got less and less.

"But Toby said it wasn't red fever," said Jamie. Toby held his breath. Would his dad be mad that he'd said that?

"We'd thought she was immune to red fever," interrupted Toby's dad. "We thought we all were … but she's been so ill — what with the rash and the feverishness — I've been so worried. She's been getting weaker and weaker. I'm scared we're going to lose her."

"Maybe it's ME," Jamie continued.

What did he know? Was he a doctor? Jamie was the same age as Toby, but his dad was paying his opinions as much attention as if he was talking to a real doctor. Toby angrily shoved the door open.

"What are you talking about?" he asked. His dad got to his feet.

"Oh, Toby, there you are. Jamie and I were just discussing Sylvie's illness. He thinks that she might have ME, not red fever."

"And what's that?" asked Toby sulkily.

"Myalgic Encephalomyelitis. And I'm not saying that is what's she's got — just that it could be," replied Jamie.

"Eh?" Toby didn't think he could have even pronounced it, never mind known what it was.

"Apparently, we've been doing all the right things for her," said his dad.

"I'm so glad," said Toby truculently. "So how did she get this Myalgic … whatever it is?"

"Nobody really knows for certain," replied Jamie, "but another name for it is Post Viral Fatigue Syndrome, so I suppose she may have had a small dose of the virus. She had enough immunity to fight it off but it left her in a very weak state. Another theory is that a big shock can trigger it off."

It took a moment for Toby and his dad to absorb all the new information. Toby knew what his dad was thinking. Sylvie had had the biggest shock of her life — losing her mum. And whose fault was that?

"So, what do we have to find to cure her?" asked Toby's dad.

"There's not a cure, as such." Jamie turned to look at Toby. He seemed shocked when he saw the angry look on Toby's face. "She's not to be stressed or do anything tiring."

Why is he looking at me? Has Dad told him what happened? Does he know about Mum?

"It's difficult not to stress her — this life isn't exactly stress-free," sighed his dad.

"You mustn't let her pick up any infections," continued Jamie. "Her immune system is very weak, so she has no resistance to germs. If she catches even just a cold …"

"I think we know what you're trying to say," Toby interrupted. "She'll die if we don't look after her properly!"

"Now, Toby," said his dad. "That's not what Jamie said. He was only trying to say how important …"

"I know what he was trying to say, Dad!" cried Toby. He left before the tears that were pricking the back of his eyes could run down his cheeks.

He makes it sound like it's my fault that Sylvie's ill. It's all because of what happened to Mum. It was all my fault and Dad's never going to forgive me!

Toby ran up the stone steps, past his own bedroom door on the next level and then climbed the steep wooden staircase into the lamp room. He threw himself against the window, the sobs wrenching from his chest.

I hate Jamie! Why did he have to come? We were doing OK before he came. We didn't need to know what was wrong with Sylvie. We were doing the right things. He's just making Dad remember how it all started. And that it's all my fault. I hate him!

But Toby knew inside that this wasn't about Jamie. It was the thought of losing Sylvie that hurt the most. He couldn't lose her, not after losing his mum. It was too much. He burrowed his face into his arms and cried.

Stop crying, you baby. This isn't going to help. What would Mum say if she could see you now? She'd tell you to man up and get a grip! She was always so brave. She never let things get her down. She stood up to everybody.

Toby wiped his snotty wet face on his jumper, and looked out to sea. The sun was slowly dipping down behind the land to the west, throwing a pink glow on to the peaceful sea. He picked up the end of the telescope and swung it round to face inland. He could see the tiny deserted houses of the village spreading up the hillside. He could see the empty fields behind, which were once full of cattle and sheep. He could see …

What's that?

He refocused and took another look. There it was, the unmistakable movement of a dog crossing the field. Then another dog appeared, and another. Toby counted five dogs in all, crossing the field as bold as could be.

Strange, where have they come from?

The local dogs usually hunted at night, and besides which, these dogs didn't look like the ones Toby was used to seeing. The local dogs were thin, mangy-looking beasts, their long matted coats mostly white with black markings. Many of them had been farm collies at one time.

Toby scanned the fields once more. Yes, there they were. These dogs were much bigger, some had short glossy black coats, others were a mixture of brown and grey with dense curly coats. They looked healthy and fit as they jogged casually over the muddy park and down towards the village.

"Dad!" Toby screamed down the steps. "You'd better come and see this."

His dad was beside him in seconds, frantically scanning the village.

"Five dogs? You saw five dogs?" he asked.

"Yeah, and they weren't the usual mangy pack of mutts from round here," replied Toby.

"I can see them," said his dad. "They're going into the Miller's garage. They won't find anything to eat in there." He swung the telescope back to Toby. "Here, you keep an eye on them. I'm going to put the chickens in. I'll check the fencing and the gates too. Can't afford to make any mistakes."

Toby winced.

He meant he would check the gates because he doesn't trust me to do it after what happened to Mum.

Toby's dad ran down the stairs. Toby kept the telescope trained on the small village. He saw the dogs leave the garage and trot down the main road. They kept together, their noses not far apart, glancing from side to side as they went. Not one of them stopped to sniff a lamp-post or cock its leg on a bush. They moved as one.

"Are they black?" asked a voice behind him. Toby wheeled round. It was Jamie.

"Some of them are — the biggest ones. And they all look really fit. These are not the local dogs," replied Toby, trying hard not to feel irritated by Jamie's presence.

Jamie went over to the window and squinted out, holding his hand up to his eyes.

"I've got awful eyesight," he confessed. "Can't see a thing. I broke my specs ages ago. I'm lost without them."

"Ummm," muttered Toby, trying to feign interest.

"Tell me, what are they doing?"

"I'm not sure. They seem to be doing a reccy of the village at the moment," said Toby.

"It's exactly what Mum said," whispered Jamie, as if to himself. "The dogs are moving in organised packs out of Aberdeen and into the countryside. They're taking possession of the land and the villages. Any people left will be trapped in their homes and either starve or have to escape to find food. The dogs will rule the land and the shores."

"Yeah, yeah," jeered Toby. "And I suppose this Cerberus is going to be crowned king of all the dogs!"

"You're probably closer to the truth than you realise," replied Jamie.

"Here, you keep watch." Toby swung the telescope over to Jamie. "Dad doesn't trust me anyway." He turned and stomped down the stairs. He would go and see if Sylvie was OK.

Sylvie was sitting in the kitchen with a big pot of crayons, drawing a clown and colouring it in.

"Do you like my clown?" she asked. "Have you ever been to the circus?"

"It's a lovely clown," said Toby, ruffling the top of her head with his bandaged hand. It wasn't nearly so sore as it had been. "No, I've never been to a circus. Mum didn't like them. But I saw clowns on the streets of Edinburgh during the festival one summer. They were on stilts. It was great!"

"Can you draw one for me?" Sylvie offered him an orange crayon. Toby sat beside her and, taking the back of an old cereal packet, started to draw an orange clown on stilts.

Sylvie rested her head on her hands and coughed a dry, scratchy cough.

"Are you all right?" Toby asked her. He put his non-bandaged hand to her head. She was hot.

"Sylve, I think it's about your bedtime, OK?" he said, taking her hand. It felt hot and sticky too. "Come on, into bed." He led her across to her makeshift day bed on the sofa. She didn't complain but crawled in and snuggled down straightaway. "I'll get you a drink of water." Toby went and fetched her a mug of cold water, but when he returned, she was fast asleep.

Toby decided to go outside and help his dad. The chickens could be skittish at times. His dad was closing the shed door as Toby walked down into the compound.

"All the ladies are safely shut up for night," said his dad, pushing the bolt shut. "I'm going to go and check the lock on that gate."

"I'll come with you. Jamie's keeping watch and Sylvie's asleep. She's running a high temperature again."

His dad nodded. "We'll need to keep an eye on that. We've run out of Calpol, and I don't dare give her any adult paracetamol, not that we've got much of that either."

"One tablet," said Toby. "Last time I looked in the first-aid tin there was just one tablet left." His dad shrugged his shoulders resignedly.

"I know, we really need to find some more medicines," he said.

The two of them swung open the heavy wooden gates of the compound. To the left was a path that led down to the jetty where the *Lucky Lady* was moored. To the right was a stony track which led along the rocky promontory up to the village. About twenty yards along this, the track narrowed and the ground fell steeply away either side of it. This was where Toby's dad had put up tall chain-link fencing that went down each side of the track and into the sea. Two massive gates stood on the track, fastened with a huge iron chain and padlock. Toby's dad went and shook them vigorously.

"They'll hold!" he cried to Toby, who was inspecting the supporting struts of the fencing. "You'd need to ram them with a tractor to get these gates down."

"These still seem solid," Toby cried back, trying to shake the posts in the ground.

He lifted his head. His eye had caught some movement in the village on the hillside above them. He frowned and squinted into the evening light. Had he imagined it? Something in the half-light darted across the play park. A baby swing swayed back and forth, creaking spookily. Toby stared into the dusk. Was it a rabbit or a hare? There were certainly hundreds of them around the area, with its surrounding fields of grass and weeds to eat. No, it had been bigger than a rabbit.

Something shot across the tarmac car park near the beach. There was more than one. Surely Jamie would have warned them if the dogs had come closer?

"Toby, come here, slowly," his dad quietly commanded.

Toby climbed back up the bank on to the track and stood beside his dad. There, coming down the track five abreast, were the dogs. They trotted calmly out of the gloom of the dusk towards them.

"Don't move!" hissed his dad.

"We're safe here, aren't we?" Toby hissed back.

"We should be. Can't see them getting over these gates, and they certainly can't get through them," said his dad.

Why am I so scared then? thought Toby. *They look like they mean business. I don't think they want us to throw them a ball!*

The dogs were getting closer. They sniffed the air and then stopped a few feet from the gates. They were tall, handsome dogs with shiny coats.

"Don't look them in the eye," said Toby's dad. "I read somewhere that that just annoys dogs."

"No," said a voice behind them. Jamie had been walking quietly towards them. "*Do* look them in the eye. Stare hard back at them. Draw yourself up to your full height and look as domineering as you can," he instructed.

"What?" gasped Toby. "I thought …"

"These are foot soldiers," interrupted Jamie. "They're not the dominant ones in the pack. They're used to being given orders. So order them to go away."

"What d'you mean?" gasped Toby's dad.

"Look," said Toby, "they're wagging their tails! Maybe they're friendly dogs."

"That's a sign that they're excited," said Jamie. "See how their tails are arched high over their backs and are wagging slowly. If they were being friendly their tails would be lower and wagging faster."

"Excited? Is that good?" hissed Toby.

"No, now on the count of three we're going to shout as loudly as we can, 'Get lost!'" ordered Jamie, moving closer to the gates. Toby and his dad followed.

"Get lost? That's it?"

"Yes, now … one — two — three!"

"GET LOST!" they all shouted together as loudly as they could.

The dogs threw back their heads and, rearing up, turned on their haunches and ran away.

"Keep shouting!" said Jamie.

"GET LOST! GET LOST! GET LOST! GET LOST!" they screamed at the retreating backs of the dogs.

"Couldn't we just have thrown something at them to make them go away?" asked Toby's dad, as they made their way back to the compound.

"Well, that would have driven them away from the gates for now, but they wouldn't have connected stuff that came randomly flying through the air with you. Standing your ground and showing them that you weren't frightened of them was a much better way of giving the message that this is your territory."

"I hope you're right, Jamie," said Toby's dad. "Come on, let's lock up for the night, and go and get some tea."

"I'll come inside in a few minutes. I just need to let Belle out and feed her," yelled Jamie as he headed for Belle's shed in the compound.

"What if they come back?" Toby asked his dad.

"We've checked the fencing — it's strong. We're safe here. They can't get in, and why would they want to? We've no fresh food, and everything in tins and packets is well hidden, so they can't have smelt that."

"No, but they would have smelt the chickens, and …" Toby watched as Belle raced around the yard after a ball that Jamie had thrown for her. He pointed to the large white dog, "… Belle."

I've a feeling those dogs will be back. And next time, shouting at them will be useless.

12. A Betrayal

A summer storm got up that night and whipped the village with a frenzied wind. Toby lay in his bed listening to the wailing and moaning of the gusts swirling around the lighthouse. Far below he could hear the crashing of waves breaking on the shore and on the rocks of the promontory. Nearby, in the room below, he heard his dad singing his mum's lullaby to Sylvie, in a sweet sing-song voice he only used with her.

Toby thought about the dogs. They had been so like the dogs in his nightmare, it was scary. What if he'd had some premonition? What if the nightmare was going to come true?

Go to sleep, he told himself, turning over. *That's mad. You're supposed to be a logical thinker — an engineer. It's just rubbish about dreams and that …*

He fell to sleep thinking about how great it would be to go to university and learn to be a real engineer, like his dad had been.

Woof! A deep bark woke him from his sleep. Belle was standing next to his bed. *Woof, woof!* She placed her paw on the duvet and scratched it back and forwards.

Toby sat up. It couldn't be that late; his candle was still sputtering in the night jar beside his bed.

"What are you doing here? You should be in your kennel," he said, yawning. The storm was still raging outside. The wind was tearing at the wooden shutters at his window, banging them back and forth.

"Come on," ordered Toby. "Let's take you back to Jamie. Downstairs with you!" He pulled an old hoodie on over his jammies, and crept down the stairs.

There was no sign of Jamie. He should have been asleep on the sofa but it was empty. Toby raced back up the stairs to the lamp room. That was the only other place he could be. The lamp room was full of the noise of the howling wind but there was no sign of Jamie.

He's not gone outside, surely? Not in this weather? And why did he leave Belle behind?

Toby craned his neck to look out of the window and down into the compound. But in the dark, with the rain lashing the glass, he couldn't see anything.

He raced in his stocking feet back down the stairs to the kitchen on the first floor of the lighthouse. To get to the ground floor and outside, Jamie would have needed to lower the wooden steps leading from the hatch in the floor of the kitchen. Toby's dad put them in as a safety measure so that they could be drawn up every night and locked. He felt safer knowing that even if someone or something got into the compound, they still couldn't get into their living quarters in the lighthouse.

The hatch in the kitchen was closed, but when Toby opened it he found that the steps had been lowered. Jamie must have gone outside.

Why? thought Toby. *Is he completely insane?*

He pulled on his wellies and went down the stairs, calling Belle to go with him. Once outside in the dark, wet night, Toby couldn't make out where Jamie had gone. He couldn't have opened the compound gates; they were heavy and awkward. Besides, did he know where Toby's dad kept the key? Toby thought not.

Suddenly Belle took off. She ran towards one of the older barns that wasn't used very often. It was full of stuff they'd stored in case it might be useful one day: old engine parts, empty oil cans, buckets without handles, coils of climbing ropes and a pair of old skis. Toby followed Belle.

The barn door stood slightly ajar. Toby slid into the

dark room, trying to make out something in gloom. There appeared to be a light coming from the back of the building. It was a tiny round beam such as that from a torch, and it was moving towards him. Then it went out abruptly. Toby stood stock still in the dark.

Someone's in here. I can feel them. I can hear them breathing.

"Jamie? Is that you?" he squeaked nervously.

Someone rammed into his side and Toby fell to the floor.

Whoever it was who had pushed him was now busy tying his hands behind his back, then his feet together. Toby felt groggy. He had hit the side of his head on the floor. It hadn't been hard, but it was enough to make him lose his balance and his bearings.

"Jamie?" he repeated. "Jamie, what are you up to?"

A light came on under Toby's chin. It lit up his face and that of the pale boy holding it.

"I'm sorry," said Jamie. "I'm really sorry to have to do this to you but I must go and find my mum."

"Yeah, well, feel free. I won't stop you. Be glad to see the back of you quite honestly. Go! And take your dog with you. See if I care. Just let me go!"

"It's not that simple," whispered Jamie. "You see, I need the *Lucky Lady*."

Toby kicked out and strained against the ropes holding him.

"You can't do that! That's the only means we have of getting away from here! We need that boat! How else are we going to get food and fuel and medicine?"

"I'll leave you the dinghy. You'll be fine. You'll be able to sail back to Peterhead harbour and find another boat. There were loads there," gabbled Jamie.

"Yeah. And loads of pirates too!" retorted Toby. "You're mad! You can't even sail that boat by yourself!"

"You don't understand. I need to find my mum. I know she's there! I know exactly where she'll be!"

"You can't know what's happened to her — she might not even be there. What if she went back to Newburgh to look for you?"

"We had a plan — a contingency plan for if things went wrong. Maggie and I were to go to a certain place at a certain time, on the same day of every month. Mum said she'd keep going there on that day until we turn up. It's simple. I need to get to Aberdeen in the next few days, or else I'll have to wait another month. And she might not sur—"

"So, this plan, you've had it a while then?" interrupted Toby.

"Yes, we've always had it."

"No, I mean this plan to steal the *Lucky Lady* and rush off on some mad rescue mission as if you're James Bond."

To Toby's surprise Jamie collapsed into tears. He let out an almighty blub and dropped the torch.

"I knew I wasn't brave enough to do this," he snorted through his tears. "I wish I was like you! You're always so brave and strong. Even when you had that septic hand, you still rescued me and Belle."

"Me? Brave?" said Toby. "I'm not brave at all. I thought you were the brave one — you never seem to be affected by anything that's going on."

"Ah, that's the influence of …"

"Oh, just stop blubbing and get these ropes off me now!" ordered Toby.

Jamie picked up the torch and untied the rough rope from Toby's wrists and ankles.

"That's better," said Toby, scratching his legs. "Now, how were you going to get out of the compound anyway? D'you know where Dad keeps the key?"

"No, I don't, but I found a hole in the wall at the back of this barn. Well, actually Belle found it," said Jamie.

"What? You found a hole in the wall? Why didn't you tell me? That changes everything!"

"What d'you mean, changes everything?" sniffed Jamie.

"You don't understand; I'll tell you sometime. I've got to find Dad." Toby jumped up and snatched the torch from Jamie.

"No!" said Jamie, snatching it back. "I told you, I must go and meet my mum. If something's happened to her, I'll never forgive myself. She might be needing me right now. I've got to go!"

"Jamie! You can't take the *Lucky Lady*. I won't let you!"

"Well, how about the dinghy then? Can I have that?" pleaded Jamie.

"No! Do you realise how dangerous it is out there? Especially in Aberdeen, from what your mum's told you. You wouldn't last two shakes of a puppy dog's tail."

"Please. Please, Toby, you've got to help me. It's my mum — I know she's in trouble. Please help. And she might be able to help you," he added. "She's a doctor; think about it …"

"Stop crying and I'll think about it," replied Toby.

This could be it — my way of saving Sylvie — if Jamie's mum is still alive …

"Let me think," said Toby, "make a plan, that sort of thing. It takes a lot of planning does a rescue mission, y'know."

"Yours didn't when you rescued me and Belle. You just jumped in the dinghy and rowed."

"Talking of Belle, where is she?" said Toby. His eyes had got used to the darkness and he couldn't see the big white dog in the barn or out in the yard.

"Belle," said Jamie anxiously. "Belle, come! Come!"

The boys heard a distant barking.

"That's not Belle," cried Jamie. "I know her bark, and that's not it."

The two boys raced out into the yard. There was no sign of Belle in the compound at all.

"Oh no!" screamed Jamie. "She's gone through the hole!"

They raced back into the barn. There, right at the back, hidden by rubbish and rusting car parts, was a small hole in the stonework of the wall. It was only big enough for a dog or a small person to go through. Jamie pushed his way through easily, but Toby had difficulty getting his middle bit through. By the time he had wriggled out on to the sandy ground on the other side, Jamie had disappeared into the night.

"Jamie!" he yelled.

Woof! A softer, sweeter bark than before, replied. Belle came running up from the direction of the jetty path.

"Where's your dad?" Toby asked the dog.

She whined and licked his hand, then shot off back down the path.

Toby followed hesitantly. The path was slippery in places and he was having difficulty seeing where to put his feet.

"Toby!" came a small voice from beside the path.

"Toby, I've fallen and twisted my ankle. Can you help me up, please?"

"Ah, you big nana! What were you doing? Making a run for the boat? Didn't you trust me?" Toby found where the voice was coming from and knelt beside Jamie's crumpled legs.

"No, I didn't."

"Well, I meant it, OK? If I say I'll do something, I mean it. My mum taught me that — she said it was integrity, or something," said Toby. "Now, lean on me and we'll get back quick before Dad wakes up."

A deep throaty bark came from nearby.

Jamie pulled himself up, leaning on Toby, and flashed the torch out towards the sea.

"Sounded like it was coming from that direction," he whispered nervously to Toby. The torchlight swept over the dancing waves. The wind was still thrashing the sea into a frenzy.

"There!" shouted Toby. "Look! Their eyes!" The light reflected back from the pale eyes of something in the water. "Quick!" he yelled. "It's the dogs! They've swum around from the beach to get to the headland."

The torch picked out three sets of gleaming eyes getting closer to the rocky shore that they stood on. Toby half carried, half dragged Jamie up the path.

"Come on! We've got to get back to the compound."

They staggered up the path towards the back of the compound wall, where the hole and safety was. Belle was nowhere to be seen.

"Belle!" Jamie cried out frantically, but the words were whipped from his mouth and lost in the wind.

"She'll have gone back," gasped Toby through the pain. Most of Jamie's weight was on his bandaged hand. They slipped and struggled across the sandy scrubland next to the compound.

"Toby, over there!" Jamie swung his torch around to face up towards the barn wall. There were three black dogs. This time, they weren't wagging their tails at all. Their hackles stood up like giant ruffs around their necks and each was baring his teeth. Toby could see the drools of slobber flecking their dark coats.

The boys stopped and stared.

"What now?" asked Toby. "You're the dog expert."

"I don't think shouting at them's going to work this time, d'you?" sobbed Jamie.

"No, perhaps not," Toby hissed.

We're going to need a miracle to get out of this.

13. Belle to the Rescue

It seemed as if they stood there for hours, staring at each other. All Toby could hear was the intense low vibrating of the dogs' growls. The wind and the rain had quietened into the background, and Jamie's whisperings were inaudible to him. His legs were stuck to the floor, and his arms were glued to his sides. This was his nightmare come true — only instead of one dog, there were three.

I bet if I tried to scream, nothing would come out.

Gradually, as if in slow motion, he became aware of a growing pain in his hand. Then he realised that Jamie was gripping on to it very tightly. The pain brought him back to what was happening.

"Keep still," he muttered under his breath. "I'll run to

the left and distract them, while you go for the hole. It's right behind them."

"No," hissed Jamie, "you'll never outrun them. I'll draw them away and you go and get help."

"There's no time. Are you ready? One — two — three!"

Toby pushed Jamie forward, and then made to run to the right, stopping in mid-flight to change direction and jumping to the left. But before he could complete his leap, something large and white leapt over the top of him and Jamie.

"Belle," Jamie sobbed.

Belle was much bigger than the dogs in front of her, but there were three of them and only one of her. She wagged her tail at them and woofed loudly. They closed their gaping mouths and stopped growling. They seemed surprised, and backed up, whining and yelping at her. Belle leapt into the air and bounced away into the darkness. The three dogs stood still for a moment and then leapt after her.

"Come on, let's get into that hole," roared Toby into Jamie's ear. Toby grabbed him, hauled him up to the wall and then shoved him through the hole. He quickly followed.

Once inside the barn again, Toby frantically searched for something to block the hole with. He passed Jamie a plank of wood.

"Here," he told him, "anything comes through that hole and you bash it on the head. Right?"

"What if it's Belle?" whined Jamie. But Toby didn't think Belle would be coming back.

The two boys sat shivering in their wet clothes beside the hole. It was dark and cold in the barn and all they could hear was the occasional barking of dogs coming from outside the compound.

"Toby? Toby? Jamie?" It was Toby's dad calling them from the yard.

"Here," said Toby, taking the plank from Jamie. "You go and fetch my dad and I'll guard the hole. You've done enough."

Actually, I think you couldn't knock the skin off a rice pudding!

"OK," said Jamie, looking relieved. He limped out to find Toby's dad. A few moments later they returned.

"What have you boys been up to?" demanded Toby's father. "What's going on?"

At that moment, a large white furry head burst through the hole.

"Ah!" screamed Toby with surprise.

"Belle!" shouted Jamie. "I didn't think I was going to see you ever again!"

Belle struggled through the hole and licked Jamie's face.

"Help me," yelled Toby. He had found an old chest freezer and was busy trying to push it up against the hole in the wall. His dad set his shoulder to the corner of the freezer and heaved. The freezer slid into place.

"You boys go inside. I'll finish off plugging this hole so nothing can get in," said his dad. Toby and Jamie limped back to the lighthouse, Belle jumping at their sides, wagging her tail.

Later they sat in the kitchen, slurping hot chocolate and discussing their fate.

"He's going to be mad with you," said Toby. "Fancy trying to nick our boat! And after I said I would help you."

"Don't tell him, please, Toby," begged Jamie. "It'll make it all the harder to go next time."

Even after their crazy night, Toby knew he was right. They had to go to Aberdeen — for Jamie's mum and for Sylvie.

"Yeah, well, we'd better not tell my dad everything. Leave it to me."

When his dad joined them, after a fumbled excuse for being outside in the first place, Toby told him all about Belle finding a hole in the wall of the barn.

"Don't you see, Dad," said Toby, "that it could have been there all the time? Monty could have got out through that hole. He was smaller than Belle."

His dad stared deep into his mug of tea, his shoulders drooped and his hands were shaking.

"I can't think at the moment, Toby, I'm tired," he muttered. "We'll talk about this in the morning. I must go back to bed and get some sleep. Sylvie's been restless tonight." He got up and walked slowly up the stairs to his room.

"I'm off to bed too," said Toby. "I expect Dad won't mind if you keep Belle in the kitchen with you tonight. She's earned it after saving our skins."

Jamie hugged Belle, who wagged her tail and grinned widely.

"She was brill, wasn't she?" he beamed.

"Yeah, she certainly was." Toby smiled at the pair of them.

He wearily climbed the stairs. His hand throbbed and his legs felt weak and watery. But he felt good. That hole had been there all the time. It hadn't been his fault that Monty had got out. And so it wasn't his fault that his mum had gone out to find him. Maybe his dad would forgive him now, see that he was trustworthy. He *had* put Monty in the barn that night, and he *had* checked him before going to bed. But he hadn't known that hole was there. No one had known, except Monty.

As he climbed the stone steps past his dad's bedroom, Toby heard a noise. He stopped and listened. It was a low, quiet sobbing. Toby knew it was his dad. Should he go in and comfort him? No, he couldn't bring his feet to walk to the door and push it open. He would leave his dad to his tears. He couldn't face it. He went to his bed.

The next morning was bright and breezy. The storm had cleared the stuffy summer air and brought a freshness back. Toby was up early and whistled as he did his chores. He tried to sneak a look in the barn where the hole was, but his dad had boarded up the door and parked an old truck firmly up against the doors. Even if anyone or anything ever found that hole again, that's as far as they were going.

Toby went in for his breakfast. He looked forward to his porridge, and if he was lucky there might be some jam or tinned fruit to have with it. His dad was sitting at the table with his head in his hands.

"How's Sylvie this morning?" asked Toby.

"Not good," mumbled his dad. "Her temperature is very high and she can barely speak for her sore throat."

This didn't seem a good time to have a talk with his dad about Monty and his mum's accident.

"Dad, why don't you let me go to Aberdeen and find some antibiotics?" he suggested. "Aren't those what she needs right now?"

"Aberdeen? No way, Toby. We need to be thinking about moving somewhere else, and hope that things will be better there."

"Where? Where would we go?"

"I don't know, Tobes," replied his dad. "Now the dogs have learnt they can get to us by swimming across to the headland, everything is going to be even more difficult. Before, we were at least able to get to the boat safely enough, and go fishing, and look for fuel and food. Now, that's going to be a nightmare."

Toby nodded. He had enjoyed the fresh fish and crab they caught on their expeditions. They made a change from tinned stuff and the endless bowls of soup his dad made from the vegetables grown in a plot inside the compound walls.

"Moving isn't going to help Sylvie right now, Dad," said Toby. "She's needs rest and medicine."

"Maybe Jamie can help?" quavered his dad. "He helped you, didn't he? Where is he?" The lack of sleep was weakening his dad. Toby could see that he was getting to a point where his responsibilities were all too much for him. And what then?

"He's outside playing with Belle," replied Toby. "I'll call him."

Jamie and Belle came bounding up the steps into the kitchen. Toby could see a change in Jamie. Toby's decision to help him find his mum had really cheered him up.

"It's a lovely day, Mr Tennant," said Jamie. "You should see what the storm has washed up on the shore. There's …"

"It's too dangerous to go and get it now," Toby's dad said gloomily. "We can't take the risk any more."

"Dad would like you to have a look at Sylvie," asked Toby. It no longer bothered him that his dad treated Jamie as an adult. Toby knew that Jamie was just as scared as he was, and perhaps not as brave.

Jamie and Toby went up to his dad's room. Sylvie was lying on his bed, tossing and turning, soaked in sweat. Her breathing came in small wheezy gasps.

"Hi Sylvie," said Toby gently, bending over her. Her breath smelt stale and unpleasant. She opened her eyes and stared at Toby as if she didn't know him.

"My throat hurts, Mummy," she whispered hoarsely.

"Sylvie? It's Toby."

"She's confused, Toby," said Jamie, placing a comforting hand on Toby's shoulder. "She's got such a high fever; it can fog people's brains."

No! No! Not Sylvie!

A cold hand of fear came over Toby. Was he going to lose Sylvie too? And with his dad in no state to think, it was up to him now.

"Can't you help her?"

"I'm really sorry, Toby, I don't know how. She's too weak. She needs proper medical care, and fast."

"But you helped me!"

"You were fit and strong. I didn't cure you. All I did was give you some herbal medicine to help you mend and relax. Your own body did the rest. Sylvie needs more than that now."

"That's it decided then. We're going to Aberdeen, tonight!" declared Toby. "And don't mention anything to my dad. He'll only try to stop us."

The two boys went back down to the kitchen. It had been decided that Jamie would spend the day secretly collecting provisions for the journey and hiding them in Belle's shed. Toby's dad would never look in there. They would need some food and fuel for the outboard motor of the dinghy. Toby had been adamant that they weren't taking the *Lucky Lady*. She was too easy for the dogs to spot from the shore, and besides, if they didn't make it back, his dad and Sylvie would need her to escape and make a new life somewhere else, without him.

I can do this! thought Toby. *I can! I just need to be big and brave this one last time and then everything will be all right.*

He knew that this mission wouldn't be the end of their problems. But if he could get help and medicine, maybe Sylvie would survive.

I'm going to think like mum did. She always said, take one problem at a time, and think about the others tomorrow.

Toby's dad had fallen asleep with his head on his hands at the table. Toby quietly shook him.

"Dad, why don't you go up and have a nap in my bedroom? I'll keep an eye on Sylvie. I'll wake you if there's any change," he whispered. His dad groggily nodded in a half-sleep.

"Come and get me if she gets any worse," he grunted, and went upstairs.

Toby spent the rest of the morning sitting on the bed beside Sylvie, planning his next mission. This one seemed even madder and more desperate than his dad's idea of searching the oil platform, hiding the *Lucky Lady* in Peterhead harbour or rescuing Jamie and Belle.

Occasionally Sylvie woke and looked at him as if he were a stranger. He kept a cold wet flannel pressed to her brow. He'd seen someone do that in an old film on the telly. Watching telly all seemed like a long time ago. Was it really only three years since the telly screens had gone blank?

"Toby!" Jamie was calling down the steps from the lamp room. He had gone up to watch for dog activity. "Toby!"

Toby carefully prised himself away from Sylvie, who was lying spread-eagled over his legs. He climbed up the steps and into the lamp room.

"What's up?" he asked Jamie, who was studying the hillside intently through the telescope.

"There's something going on with the dogs in the village. I think the cavalry has arrived," babbled Jamie.

"What you on about? Cavalry?" quizzed Toby.

"Y'know, the cavalry — reinforcements, back-up."

"Oh no!" exclaimed Toby, racing to look out of the tall window.

There on the hillside, sitting in the kids' playground, was a big pack of dogs. There were more than five this time. They were sitting sniffing the air and watching the main road into the village, as if they were waiting for something to happen.

"They're waiting for Cerberus," Jamie quietly stated.

"How d'you know that?" asked Toby.

"Watch, there's something coming down the road now." Jamie nervously polished the eyeglass to the telescope.

Toby peered into the distance. There, strutting down the middle of the road, came a massive black dog. Flanking him, as if they were his bodyguards, were two huge brown dogs with long pointy noses. The other dogs waiting by the swings all stood up and wagged their tails in greeting. The big black dog slowly sat down in the centre of them. Toby and Jamie saw each of the underling dogs, one at a time, greet him. Each dog approached him with its head lowered and its ears drooping down, its muzzle turned sideways and its lip curled as if smiling. Then each dog rolled on its back, exposing the soft skin of its belly to the black dog, which sat immobile through the whole thing.

"They are showing that they accept his dominance," said Jamie, as the two boys watched, fascinated. "It's like bowing to a king. They are lower-ranking dogs, and they know their place."

"What happens now?" said Toby.

"I don't know. This is weird," replied Jamie. "I wish my mum was here; she would know. That's definitely Cerberus, though. I recognise him from my mum's description."

"Right," said Toby, "we're going *now*. As soon as we can get all the stuff into the boat, we're off. If Cerberus is here, that means the dog pack in Aberdeen is without its leader. This is the best time to go. Come on!"

The two boys sped as quietly as they could down the steps and out of the lighthouse. Toby scribbled a quick note for his dad, before taking the key to the compound gates and closing the hatch door behind him. Jamie and Belle were waiting for him by the gates. Jamie was carrying a rucksack, the contents of which he showed to Toby: a map, some food, a torch and the telescope from the *Lucky Lady*.

"Hey, when did you get that?" asked Toby.

"I stole it when your dad was carrying you in from the boat, after you'd collapsed," Jamie said sheepishly.

"What a cheek — fancy nicking stuff from a mate!" Toby smiled at the nervous-looking boy. Jamie smiled back.

He's not so bad, after all, thought Toby. *And Belle will come in useful. At least we'll have some protection.* He had wished he was going on his own, but now the mission was about to get underway, he was glad the two of them were coming with him.

The compound gates squeaked loudly as the boys pushed them slightly open and squeezed through. Toby's eyes went to his bedroom window near the top of the lighthouse. Had his dad heard? Or was he still sleeping? Toby locked the gates behind him then threw the keys through the gates, as hard as he could back towards the lighthouse door. If they had forgotten anything, it was too late now. There was no going back.

14. Real Heroes

Toby scanned the headland for any sign of the dogs, as the boys dragged the cans of fuel and the heavy rucksack down to the jetty. Belle gambolled beside them, delighting in this new game. As the summer's day heated up, the sun had warmed the sea and a grey misty haar rolled towards the village.

Ideal, thought Toby. *Just what we need. We can sneak out under this mist and the dogs won't spot us. I bet they're keeping watch from the cliffs.*

The dinghy sat tied to the jetty. Toby climbed in and started to stow the two cans of fuel in the bow.

"Hup!" Jamie commanded Belle, who with one great leap sprang into the boat.

"Watch out!" hissed Toby as the large dog thumped

down beside him. He lost his balance and grabbed hold of the side of the boat, which rocked violently. A can of fuel slipped from his grasp and fell into the water. Toby lunged to save it but was too late. It had sunk.

"Ah, no!" he gasped. "We'll not have enough fuel to get home now!"

"I'm sorry," said Jamie, climbing in beside Belle. "Shall I go and get some more?"

"No, you can't. I've locked the gates and we can't get back in," snapped Toby.

It's all going wrong already and we haven't even left the jetty!

"Is there any on the *Lucky Lady*?" Jamie asked.

"No, Dad never leaves any onboard in case someone tries to steal the boat," replied Toby sullenly. Why hadn't he decided to go on his own, after all? "Let's get going. We'll find some in Aberdeen. There must be lots in the harbour. There'll be storage tanks somewhere."

Jamie slipped the rope from the mooring, then he and Toby swapped places so Toby could operate the outboard motor. The dinghy drifted quietly away from the shore.

Toby stood up and gripped the starter cord. He pulled hard on it. It had to start first time. They couldn't take the risk of the dogs being alerted to them leaving. They had seen that the dogs were powerful swimmers and wouldn't stop at following them into the water. The engine whined and then roared into action.

Yes! We're away!

Toby swung the tiller over to push the nose of the dinghy out towards the grey banks of fog rolling in from the sea. The dinghy bumped steadily over the waves, heading south-east.

"What's that?" cried Jamie, holding hard on to Belle. His face was taut with fear. Through the haar came a growing cacophony of yelps and whines, gruff barking and howling. The dinghy was passing close to the cliffs which jutted out south of the village.

"The dogs!" Jamie yelled over the roar of the motor.

Toby looked up to where he was pointing. Through the scudding clouds on the top of the cliffs they could make out a pack of large dogs jumping around excitedly. The dogs had seen the dinghy and were desperate to get to them. As the dinghy sailed away from the cliffs, taking a course parallel to the sands on the other side, the dogs took off at a gallop. A flurry of tails and flying limbs cascaded down the steep path to the beach.

"Speed up a bit, can't you, Toby?" croaked Jamie. "They're coming fast!"

When Toby half-turned to see how close the pack was, he caught a glimpse of one lone dog standing still at the top of the cliff. It was Cerberus.

They watched the dogs following them along the beach, screaming and yapping, until the small boat pulled away from the shoreline to clear the next headland. The noise receded into the distance as the mist swirled around them.

"Not good," Jamie sighed. "That was not good, eh, Belle?" He patted her. She had been strangely quiet since they left the jetty.

"Belle must be the only one of us who's putting any weight on," observed Toby. "I'm sure she's got fatter in the few days she's been with us."

Jamie gave him a strange look.

"What is it?" asked Toby. It now seemed obvious there was something Jamie wasn't telling him.

"She's having puppies," he said. "That's why that man wanted to kill her. He was scared she was going to have wild puppies, like those dogs."

"Puppies?" Toby smiled. "Sylvie loves puppies. She'll be so happy."

"I thought Sylvie hated dogs," said Jamie.

"Only big, grown-up dogs. And that's because …"

"Because of what happened to your mum?" interrupted Jamie.

"I don't want to talk about it," said Toby curtly, turning his head to stare out to sea.

The journey continued in silence as the dinghy bounced and bobbed down the coastline. Toby knew that as long as they didn't stray far in the mist, they couldn't get lost.

Aberdeen was more or less due south of Collieston. He kept his eye on the map, though, ticking off places in his mind as they passed them. They were soon crossing the side current from where the estuary at Newburgh flowed out into the sea. Hundreds of ducks were bobbing on the waters close to the shore.

"Those are eider ducks," Jamie told him, pointing to a group of fluffy-looking brown half-grown chicks. "They used to use their feathers for stuffing duvets and pillows."

Toby nodded. *Just what I always wanted to know!*

But he couldn't help smiling. Here they were, two boys and a dog cruising along in a dilapidated old rubber dinghy, heading towards what was probably a complete disaster, and all Jamie could talk about was stuffing pillows with duck feathers.

The light was starting to go early, with the cold mist still sitting on the east coast. The boys pulled on an extra jumper each and their waterproofs as the dampness crept into their bones.

"Do we need to camouflage ourselves?" Jamie broke the silence. "Y'know, put mud on our faces or something?"

"Mud is hardly camouflage for a city, is it?" scoffed Toby. "I'd be more worried about Belle — she sticks out like a sore thumb." Jamie sat quietly for a while.

"I've been thinking," he said eventually. "What if we shave her fur off and put oil all over her?"

"She'll look like a body builder then. What's the point in that?" chortled Toby.

They were now cruising past the giant dunes that spilled out on to the clean white sands of Balmedie. The wreck that Toby and his dad had seen almost a year ago was still sitting up from the sand. But now more of it had been sucked into the seabed and only the rusted bow remained.

Jamie passed Toby a boiled egg and a carrot. "Got to keep your strength up!" he said, trying to smile cheerily.

Toby was beginning to feel sick. There was a tight knot in the base of his stomach, and when he tried to swallow, the pieces of egg got stuck in his throat. His head pounded with a dull beat, and his hand had started to throb too.

I bet real heroes don't feel like this before an adventure.

He pulled back on the throttle, and the boat idled in the water. They were approaching the Don estuary now and the cross-current was bouncing them around.

"What have we stopped for?" asked Jamie. "Are we there?" He peered through the murky light.

"Yeah, nearly. It might be better if we row from here in. If anyone or anything is on the lookout, we don't want to go roaring up the beach," said Toby. He reached down and passed an oar to Jamie.

"Now remember, we have to row together or else we'll

just go round in circles," he told him. "Now, one — two — three … PULL!"

The dinghy lurched forward, listing precariously to Jamie's side.

"Get Belle to sit in the middle, can you? She's capsizing the boat!"

Jamie pulled the dog into the middle and pushed her bottom down. "Sit. Sit there. Good girl."

The boat bounced across the estuary opening and followed the line of the beach, creeping slowly towards the harbour. The towering skyscrapers of Aberdeen dotted beyond the sandy links pushed their heads above the mist.

"I recognise this," said Jamie. "We're nearly there. We need to be at the beach promenade. There's a café there called the Inversneckie. My mum and I used to go there every Sunday. She'd have a skinny latte and I'd have a banana smoothie."

"Yes, well, you can spare me the details. Tell me where it is — can you remember?" Toby panted as he threw his weight on to the oar. "Keep rowing, Jamie. Never mind the trip down memory lane!"

"It's past a really old building called The Ballroom, or something," he replied, struggling to speak and row. The boat was making no headway in the tossing swell.

"I think we'd better dump the boat and walk the rest

of the way," grunted Toby. "We're not getting very far." He dropped his oar to his lap and let the boat glide towards the bank of sand at the foot of the beach. The rubber dinghy slid on to the wet shingle, and Toby jumped out.

"Out you get," he whispered to Jamie. "I'm not pulling you and that fat dog up the beach."

Toby and Jamie dragged the boat up over the sand and on to a large bank of pebbles under the beach promenade, whilst Belle picked up large pebbles with her teeth and threw them at the boys.

"We haven't got time to play now, Belle," chided Toby, as a large pebble bounced off his foot. He took a long chain and rope out of the dinghy and secured the boat to the railings that ran along the granite wall, separating the walkway from the beach. He took out the telescope and pointed it inland.

"It's hard to see anything in this mist," he said, "but there looks like a funny-shaped building further down. We'd better keep down here, below this wall. Let's go."

The other two filed behind him as they walked down the side of the beach wall, along the stony shingle. They had to go slowly. The stones cracked and banged beneath their feet, making noises which, in the still air, sounded like canons going off.

After a while, Toby crawled up some steps to see if

they were anywhere near the building. He came back to where Jamie and Belle were crouching on the pebbles.

"Yeah, we're about ten metres past it. How much further d'you think this café is?" Toby asked.

"Not far. There used to be an amusement arcade on the corner and then there's a row of cafés. It's one of them," answered Jamie, who was shaking with cold and fear.

Toby glanced at his grey frightened face, peering from an oversized woolly hood, and smiled.

"It's going to be all right, Jamie," he reassured him. "We're nearly there. And think, your mum might be waiting for you!"

Jamie smiled wanly back.

Ummm, can see I'm going to have to be the strong one here, thought Toby.

They climbed the next set of steps up from the beach on to the wide path that swept along the beachfront. Ahead of them was a line of semi-derelict single-storey buildings. Most of them used to be cafés or ice-cream parlours, but now they were boarded up with bits of plywood and metal bars across the windows. The boys and Belle crossed the road to get a closer look. The faded signs over the doors said: The Blue Water Café, Harry's Fish and Chip Café, and then …

"Here it is!" exclaimed Toby. "Jamie, this one's the Inversneckie Café. It's here!"

The boys tried to peer inside the grimy door. The door had been broken and the sign saying OPEN fluttered in the breeze through the smashed glass. Toby pushed the door but it was locked from inside.

"Let's go round the back and see if we can get in there," he suggested. They trooped round behind the row of cafés to a tarmac car park, where empty bins rolled around in piles of rubbish. Toby counted the doors.

"It was the third one in from the right," he told Jamie. "This must be it." He pointed to a filthy back yard. A dirty green door was half hidden under the mounds of soggy cardboard and empty coke cans. Toby pushed his way through to the door and pushed it hard. It swung open slowly.

Inside the café kitchen, the cold dark air smelt fusty and of something long since dead.

"Poo!" retorted Toby. "Wouldn't pass a hygiene inspection now, would it?"

Jamie didn't laugh at his joke, but stared around in dismay. "Doesn't look like she's been here, does it?" he moaned.

"She's not likely to have brought her rubber gloves and given it a spring clean, is she?" remarked Toby. He looked around at the mess. It was like everywhere else these days, a clutter of rubbish and junk.

"Well, let's make ourselves comfy; we might have a

long wait. What time were you supposed to be here?" asked Toby.

"Er, well, now. I think it was midday, but I might be wrong. It is the sixth of June today, isn't it?"

"No, it's the fifth today," groaned Toby. "I know that because it's Sylvie's birthday in two days time, and I want to be back for that."

The chances of us getting back at all are looking pretty slim. This nutter doesn't even know what day it is!

"Oh, is that right?" said Jamie in surprise. "We'll have to wait until tomorrow at twelve noon to see if she's coming in that case."

"OK, we'll have to wait here," said Toby. "We'll take it in turns to keep watch, while the other one sleeps. I'll go first. You find somewhere to bunk down."

Jamie pulled out some cardboard boxes from a cupboard, climbed into the biggest one and curled up inside it. Toby positioned himself behind the counter of the café. From there he could see the back door of the kitchen, and if he peered round he could see the front door.

This is going to be a long wait, he thought. *I hope Jamie's mum shows up. Then I've got to see if she can help us and find some medicine for Sylvie. And then I've got to find us some fuel to get home. And then I've got to get us all home safely.*

Toby sighed. It all seemed totally impossible.

15. The Trail Begins

Toby was dreaming a delightful dream. He was walking on the beach with his mum and Monty, and baby Sylvie was toddling across the sand screaming with delight as the waves licked at her bare toes. He was eating a huge ice cream with a big fat chocolate flake stuck in it. The sun was hot on the back of his neck …

"Belle!" Toby woke up to find Belle licking the back of his neck.

"Toby, wake up. It's nearly twelve o'clock," Jamie whispered in his ear.

"Huh?" said Toby groggily. He sat up, slowly stretching his stiff legs. He'd fallen asleep as the sun peeped into the café, when Jamie came to take over keeping watch. Toby had sat up all night, crouched behind the counter, his nerves jumping at any faint scratching in the dark. But it was only mice scurrying across the floor, scavenging for crumbs. He hadn't wanted to wake Jamie, who'd looked so peaceful curled up in his cardboard box, Belle standing guard over him, so he'd taken his turn too.

"I'm starving!" said Jamie, digging deep into the rucksack and pulling out two old cereal bars. He tore the wrapper off one and handed Toby the other.

"Don't get too excited." Toby smiled. "These will be as fusty as hell!" He bit into his and wrinkled up his nose. "Yuk."

Jamie didn't seem to mind. He couldn't keep still and was bouncing around like a rubber ball. He packed and repacked the rucksack about ten times before Toby told him to calm down.

"Your mum might be ages. She might have problems getting out of the city and down here to the beach. If I remember, to get here she'll have to cross a large open playing field if she's coming from the town centre."

"Maybe she's already down at the beach," babbled Jamie, his eyes darting to the back door and then to the front door of the café.

"Maybe," said Toby, unconvinced.

This is such a long shot. I really don't think his mum is going to turn up.

Twelve o'clock came and went. Then one, then two,

and at five o'clock Toby knew she wasn't coming.

"We'd better get going," he announced, grabbing his cagoule. "I need to find some medicine before that dog, that Cerberus, whatever you call him, gets back to Aberdeen."

"No! Please wait a bit longer," begged Jamie. "I know she's coming! I can feel it!"

"I'm sorry, Jamie," said Toby, "but I don't think she is, and I need to complete my mission. I need to get medicine for Sylvie. You know that, you saw how ill she is, and I don't want to get home and find we're too late."

"No, I know you don't. But please! Just one more hour?" pleaded Jamie, clutching at Toby's arm. Toby could see the panic and fear in Jamie's face as it crumpled up and tears rolled down his cheeks.

"OK, OK, you win," he replied. "One more hour and that's it, I'm off. OK?"

"Yeah, OK, Toby, that's great. She'll be here, I know she will."

Jamie slumped down behind the counter, looking at his watch. Five minutes later he looked at his watch again. Toby sat down beside him.

"Look, I found an old menu," he said, trying to distract Jamie. "Hey, they used to serve knickerbocker glories. Wow! They were my favourite. My mum always bought me one on my birthday. D'you remember all that sticky gunk that used to be on the top? And sprinkles? Ummm! I can almost taste it."

"My mum would never let me have one; said they were bad for my teeth."

"Yeah, that's probably why I was only allowed one on my birthday," said Toby. "Mind you, my mum would have a fit if she could see my teeth now." He pulled open his mouth to show Jamie his yellowing, chipped teeth. "I wish she could see them, though," he finished sadly.

"I'm really sorry, 'bout your mum." Jamie patted Toby's shoulder.

"Me too," sighed Toby. "She was great fun. Totally kooky. I mean, as mad as … as …" He started to weep, the tears welling up and spilling down his dirty face. Sobs wracked his chest and he buried his head into his knees. He didn't want Jamie to see him like this.

Pull yourself together, Toby. Stop it! Stop crying, you big baby!

Jamie stuffed a filthy grey hankie into his hand.

"Thanks," Toby mumbled, dabbing his eyes, but the tears wouldn't stop.

"What happened?" Jamie asked quietly.

"She fell. She fell off the cliffs near the lighthouse," murmured Toby. "She went out to find Monty. She must have heard him barking outside the compound. Dad thought I'd forgotten to put him in the barn that night.

But he must've got out through that hole Belle found. Dad turned the lighthouse lamp on and shone it on the shore. But it was already too late; she'd slipped and fallen in the dark. It was just a terrible accident. The dogs soon started to gather at the commotion, barking; that's all me and Sylvie can remember — the terrible barking and the snarling dogs ..."

"That must have been horrible," said Jamie.

"Yes, it was," sobbed Toby.

The two boys sat in silence, Toby clutching the hankie to his nose, and Jamie with his arms around Belle. The light in the café started to fade, throwing long shadows against the walls. After a while, Toby stood up and picked up the rucksack. He turned to Jamie.

"I'm sorry, but I really must get going. Sylvie's depending on me," he said.

"I know. I'm coming with you," said Jamie, pulling himself up.

"I'll go and have a look," Toby told him. "See if it's safe to cross that playing field."

Jamie nodded. "Take Belle with you," he suggested. "She'll let you know if there are any dogs around."

Toby climbed out the back door of the café, scanning the car park before sneaking down the sides of the buildings. Belle padded quietly at his side. He listened carefully but all he could hear was the distant breaking of the waves on the beach. He swung back on to the beachfront promenade and round the side of the amusement arcade. In front of him lay a large open area of grass to cross. This was the dangerous part. There was no cover and they would be visible for miles. As the soft pink light of dusk bathed the seafront, Toby saw something on the ground. It was a large arrow, spray-painted on to the pavement, pointing towards a children's play park. Toby stared at it, puzzled.

That's strange; the paint looks fresh. Looks like it's not been there long.

He bent down to inspect the arrow closer, glancing around to check for any dogs. Belle stood obediently at his side, sniffing the air. Along the shaft of the arrow, somebody had sprayed the initials KM.

Toby turned and ran back to the café, hugging the shadows of the buildings as he went. He burst in through the back door, leaping over the heaps of rubbish.

"Jamie! Come and look at what I've found!" he cried. Jamie was standing by the front door, watching for his mum.

"What? What is it?" he gasped, surprised by Toby's quick return.

The two boys hurried back to where the arrow was painted on the pavement.

"KM — that's Katie McTavish!" yelped Jamie. "She's

still alive! I told you! And this is her leaving us a trail to help us find her!"

"Keep your voice down," Toby hissed. "We don't know what's around here. And, anyway, this doesn't prove anything. She was here, yes, but why isn't she here now?"

"I don't know, do I?" Jamie rasped back. "But I do know that I'm going to follow this arrow."

"I'm coming with you," declared Toby.

The arrow pointed across the road towards a car park. The boys crouched down and crossed the road quickly. There was another arrow sprayed in the middle of the car park. This one pointed to a hedge that bordered the edge of a children's play park. The once manicured green lawns of the park were now like a prairie, full of thick swaying grasses.

"How would she have managed to paint on grass?" quizzed Toby. "You wouldn't see the paint; the grass is too tall."

"She didn't need to — look!" Jamie pointed to a line of red that stretched from the car park down through the play park and towards a paddling pool that sat in a dip. On closer inspection, the red line was made of torn cotton strips tied in a line to the tall tops of the browning weeds.

"She's torn up a jumper or something to make markers with," observed Toby.

"I remember that hoodie," remarked Jamie. "It was her favourite."

"Your mum wears hoodies?" said Toby.

"Yeah, well, she's never been interested in clothes. Always too busy," Jamie replied.

They pressed into the waist-high grasses, stooping down and pushing the tickly thistles and dry nettles from under their noses. Belle sneezed as thousands of seeds burst from their pods and filled the air with white fairy filaments.

"Shush!" both the boys warned her.

They crept along, collecting the red cotton as they went. They didn't want anybody else following the trail.

Not that that's likely, thought Toby. *We're probably the only people mad enough to come into Aberdeen, apart from Jamie's mum.*

The trail ended at the paddling pool, the once turquoise bottom of which had turned a disgusting black-green with slime and stagnant rainwater. Belle sniffed at the broken bottles littering the edge.

"Come away, Belle," ordered Jamie. "You'll cut your paws."

"Now what?" Toby asked, searching the ground for more arrows.

"There!" exclaimed Jamie, pointing at a pile of coke cans.

"It's a pile of coke cans, you nana," said Toby.

"It's a cairn," said Jamie triumphantly. "Like you get on top of mountains. It shows we're here. This is it."

"What?" gasped Toby. "This is it? A smelly paddling pool?"

"Yeah, whatever it is, it must be around here somewhere." Jamie started to rummage round the back of a derelict shed that had been the changing rooms and toilets. Toby squatted down and kept his ears open for any signs of dog activity.

After a few minutes he became sore and stood up briefly. Jamie peered round the side of the shed and motioned Toby to follow him.

There, hidden in nettles at the back of the shed, was a large concrete lid. Someone had levered open one edge and left a metal rod in one side to keep it open.

"Come on! This must be the start of the tunnel my mum was talking about," gabbled Jamie.

"That wouldn't make sense, Jamie." Toby wasn't so sure. Why would a tunnel start there? "It's more likely to be ventilation or a maintenance shaft."

"Give me a hand," gasped Jamie, trying to lift the heavy lid.

"Use the lever," urged Toby. "That's what your mum's left it there for, you noodle!"

"Oh, yeah," said Jamie. "I was just wondering how my mum had managed to open and close this on her own."

The boys levered the lid off the concrete collar on which it was sat, and peered down into the dark hole. Jamie pulled his torch out of the rucksack and, giving it a good wind first, shone it into the shaft.

"It's not far to the bottom, actually," he said, his voice echoing in the tunnel below. "I think between us we'll be able to manhandle Belle down the ladder. Come on, Belle!" Belle wagged her tail furiously and poked at him with her nose.

"Hang on!" cried Toby. "I'm not going down there with you. I need to be going towards King Street, which I think is over that direction." He swung his arm over to the right. "I remember Dad telling me that the Offshore Survival Centre is somewhere on King Street. There might still be supplies there."

Jamie started to climb down the thin metal rungs lining the inside of the shaft.

"Please help me with Belle first, and then you can go. OK?" he said.

"OK," agreed Toby. He pushed Belle towards the hole, but she braced herself against him and stood still, her whole body rigid.

"Come on! Hurry up!" Jamie's muffled voice called from down in the tunnel.

But Belle wouldn't shift. She lifted her head to the air and sniffed deeply. A low growl rumbled in her chest.

"Er, Jamie? I think you'd better come up here. She's acting funny," called back Toby.

Jamie's head popped out of the top of the tunnel. "Get in!" he commanded Toby. "Get in the tunnel now!"

Toby didn't wait. Whatever Jamie had seen, it must be bad.

"Belle! Come!" Jamie ordered.

Belle leapt towards the shaft, and Jamie grabbed hold of her collar. "Grab her back end and push!" he yelled at Toby.

Toby did as he was told, bundling the white furry bottom into the mouth of the shaft.

Belle wriggled and then jumped down into the passageway, past Jamie. Toby hauled the concrete lid half-closed then slipped backwards on to the rungs of the ladder inside. He grabbed the metal bar to lever the lid shut and, pitting all his strength against it, heaved on it. As he did so, he caught a glimpse of a pack of dogs trotting down the beach promenade towards them. A huge black dog strutted majestically at the head of the pack.

Cerberus was back.

16. King of the Dogs

The lid was heavy and slid slowly across the gap. Jamie appeared alongside Toby and threw his weight into levering it shut. There was no time to lose. If the dogs found the entrance open, they would follow them into the tunnel.

"Push!" yelled Toby, bracing his feet against the sides of the tunnel. The lid scraped shut.

"Phew," panted Toby. "D'you think they saw us?"

"I'm not sure. But they knew we were around here somewhere. They must have followed the boat from the cliffs as we sailed down here. It seems too much of a coincidence that they came back to the city and turned up in the same place as us," whispered Jamie, sliding down the steps to the bottom of the shaft. He flashed his torch around the tunnel, which was lined with small granite cobbles. There seemed to be a faint light coming from somewhere to their right.

"I think this tunnel goes out to the beach that way," Toby said quietly. "If this was part of the sewers, that would make sense. They didn't bother treating it in the old days. They just opened the tanks at high tide and — *whoosh* — out it all went."

"Er, that's disgusting," said Jamie, wrinkling up his nose. "Oh, what's this?" Tied at the bottom of the ladder was an old plastic bottle full of a yellowy liquid. The initials KM were sprayed on it. "I think mum meant us to use this," he suggested. He took the lid off and squeezed the bottle at the ground. The yellow liquid squirted out with a pungent smell.

"Oh, that stinks!" hissed Toby.

"This must be the badger juice my mum's been using to throw the dogs of the scent. Maybe we should spray ourselves with it."

"Must we?" whispered Toby. "It's vile. Why don't you spray it at the bottom of the shaft in case they find their way up the tunnel from the beach?"

Jamie squirted the solution over the surrounding ground and their feet, including the soles of their boots.

"Hey! Belle, what are you doing?" grunted Jamie. Belle was rolling in a revolting, sticky puddle of mud and sludge. "Ah, good girl."

"What *is* she doing?" asked Toby, watching in disbelief as Belle's white fur turned to brown and then black with goo.

"Well, I think she's camouflaging herself, but *she* probably thinks she's putting on her war paint," Jamie told him. "Dogs often roll in fox poo or something yucky and really smelly. Makes them feel more dominant, so other dogs will treat them like a higher-ranking dog."

"Nice!" commented Toby. "We should be moving. Let's go."

"If we head up this tunnel on the left, it should take us into the city centre. Come on," said Jamie, throwing the light from his torch ahead of them into the dark cavern. It was broad enough for the two of them to walk side by side, with Belle trotting behind, and tall enough for them to stand upright without stooping.

"Doesn't smell that bad, considering," remarked Jamie, clasping the torch with one hand and Toby's sleeve with the other.

"Can't smell anything other than the pong of that badger juice," said Toby, rubbing his nose with the dirty hankie Jamie had given him.

They could only walk slowly along the cavern as its cobbled floor was slimy and slippery with green algae. Its walls glistened with water, and fronds of ferns and foliage sprouted out between the stones. The boys could hear the echo of their own feet as they trudged along the tunnel. They felt the floor tilting underfoot as it led them up the hill into the city centre, making it harder to keep from slipping. Every now and then they stopped to listen.

"Think what it must have sounded like when there were cars and lorries on the roads above here," said Toby. "I can remember coming into Aberdeen to see Santa at a big store one Christmas. It was so busy, we couldn't find anywhere to park, and my mum nearly gave up and went home again. But I cried and she parked on a double yellow line and got a parking ticket. But I got to see Santa. He gave me a Playmobil fire engine. I've still got it somewhere."

"My mum never believed in doing all that Santa stuff," sighed Jamie. "She thinks parents shouldn't tell their children stories like that."

"Oh, well, I suppose she might be right," said Toby. "You still got presents though?"

"Yes, one. We had one each," replied Jamie. "I wanted a computer one year but I got this wind-up torch instead."

"Hey, never mind, what does it matter?" Toby nudged him with his elbow. "Tellies and computers are not much good to us now, eh? We'd never have managed without that torch, so …"

"Shush!" Jamie held his finger to his lips. "Can you

hear that? I thought I heard a tapping noise." Toby listened to the dripping of the water and scampering of tiny feet on the wet ground.

"That's rats, that is," he told Jamie. "I hope they haven't super-evolved too. I didn't like them to start with!"

"No, not *that* noise. The one I can hear is more like a regular tapping — listen."

Belle whined and pushed at Jamie with her wet nose.

"Yeah, you can hear it too, girl, can't you?" said Jamie.

Toby listened again. Very faintly, in the distance, there was a *tap, tap, tap*. Then it stopped and then it started again: *tap, tap, tap*.

"Could just be a loose tile banging in the wind," Toby said, shrugging his shoulders. Jamie looked unconvinced.

They trudged on, skidding and sliding as the tunnel grew steeper and steeper, and the ground more slippery. They stopped to catch their breath. Ahead the tunnel split into two.

"Which way?" asked Toby. "The left tunnel or the right?"

"I don't know," said Jamie, swinging his torch in the direction of the left tunnel. "Maybe my mum's left another clue?" He pointed the light at the floor. "There's some more red cotton, here," he cried, "but it looks like the water has moved it. It could have been pointing at either of these tunnels."

Toby knelt down and studied the strips of red cloth. They lay wet and crumpled in a small pile.

"We'll just have to take a guess," he said. "Unless Belle knows?"

Belle was standing with her nose pointing down the right-hand tunnel. Her tail was wagging slowly and her ears were pricked. She gave a short whine and looked at Jamie.

"What is it, Belle?" Jamie turned to Toby. "Looks like the right tunnel's the one of choice."

The boys quickly followed Belle along the right tunnel, which became less steep and soon levelled out.

"Did your mum say what happened to the tunnel once it got to Marischal College?" asked Toby. "I mean, does it come out in the cellars? Or into the street?"

"I don't know; she never told me," replied Jamie. "Wait, I can hear that tapping again."

"You and your flipping tapping!" said Toby. But it did seem that the tapping was getting louder. Belle was bounding ahead now, going so fast that the boys had trouble keeping up with her.

"Slow down, Belle," called Jamie as she disappeared round a corner in front of them. "We don't know what's round the next bend."

They chased after her, coming round the corner in hot pursuit, but there was no sign of her. In front of them was a pile of rubble that, in the flash of Jamie's torchlight, looked like it filled the tunnel from top to bottom.

"Whoa!" yelled Toby. "The roof of the tunnel must have collapsed. But where's Belle?"

"Maybe she's under all that," cried Jamie tearfully.

"No, this isn't a fresh fall of rocks," Toby told him. "Here, give me the torch. You see how the dust has settled — if this had just happened the air would be thick with it."

"I'm so glad I've come with an engineer," Jamie whispered, half to himself.

"There must be a gap somewhere, and it won't be a small one cos Belle managed to get through," said Toby.

"Belle? Belle? Come, Belle!" Jamie called his dog.

There was a scrabbling, and some rocks and stones fell from the top of the rubble. A dirty half-black, half-white dog's head poked out from behind a large boulder near the ceiling. With a mighty wriggle, Belle jumped down and raced towards them.

"Belle, I'm so glad to see you!" sniffed Jamie, hugging the dusty dog.

She whined and ran back to the mound of rocks, then back to Jamie. She gave a short bark and jumped up at him.

"Quiet, Belle, we don't want the dogs to know where we are," Toby told her, but Belle continued to whine and run backwards and forwards.

"She wants us to go with her," said Jamie.

"Well, we've not got much choice," quipped Toby, starting to climb up the mound of rubble. His feet slipped and slid as he clutched at the crumbly rocks and pulled himself slowly to the top.

Jamie trained the light from his torch on the spot where Belle had appeared. Belle jumped up past Toby and squeezed through a crevice between two big boulders.

"Jamie, there's light coming from the other side," Toby called softly.

Jamie hitched the rucksack up on his back and climbed up beside him. They perched on the chalky broken stones and peered through the cleft in the rocks. From somewhere, clear natural light was flooding into the tunnel on the other side.

"I can hear that tapping noise again," said Jamie.

"So can I," agreed Toby. He flattened himself against the rock and then crawled through the small space leading to the other side.

The tunnel on the other side was bigger and opened into a chamber with a vaulted ceiling. The light was coming through a glass panel in the roof of a tunnel to the left of the main chamber. Toby stood underneath it and looked up.

That's weird, that's SO weird. I remember this place, but where is it?

Looking up through the glass Toby could see a room. It was covered in cobwebs but he could still make out paintings and a coat of arms on the wall, complete with a swag of tartan cloth that hung limply, heavy with dust. Toby stared and stared. The scene was like an old black and white photograph that had grown brown and faded with age. It reminded him of something.

"I remember," he muttered. "I've been in that room. It's a café. It's in Provost Skene's House. That's right — there was a pane of glass set into the floor. You could look down and see the chamber below. I went there with Mum and I wouldn't walk across the glass cos I was scared I might fall through it!"

"I know where the tapping's coming from!" exclaimed Jamie, appearing beside him.

"I know where we are!" said Toby. "We must be right under the road in front of Marischal College."

"Never mind that now," cried Jamie. "That tapping's coming from behind another pile of rocks at the end of this chamber.

Toby followed Jamie to the bank of pebbles and stones. He could hear now a distinct distant *tap, tap, tap*. He picked up a stone and tapped it hard on the wall of the chamber. *Tap, tap, tap … tap, tap, tap.*

There came a reply: *tap, tap, tap … tap, tap, tap.*

"It's Mum; I know it is!" Jamie screamed in delight.

"Hush," said Toby. "She must be stuck behind these rocks. But why doesn't she use another exit. By my reckoning, she must be in the tunnels that go under Marischal College, so why doesn't she get out that way?"

"I don't know. What are we going to do? I don't know what to do!" babbled Jamie.

"Shush for a sec. Let me think," urged Toby. "You start to make a hole through the rubble here, but be careful. It might not be stable. Watch for any loose stones. And I'll go up through Provost Skene's House and try to reach her by going through the College. OK?" Jamie nodded. "Right, first I'll need you to give me a leg up."

Jamie stood under the glass panel in the floor of Provost Skene's House, with Toby on his shoulders. "Hurry up," he cried, "I can't hold you much longer." Toby was trying to lift the pane of glass.

"Hold still!" Toby ordered. "I can't do it with you jumping all over the place." He grunted, and with one final effort the glass sprung up out of the panel and fell sideways on to the floor of the café.

"That's it," said Toby. "One last push up and I'll jump. One, two, three!" Toby launched himself upwards as Jamie pushed him up off his shoulders.

"Are you OK?" Jamie asked as Toby dangled from the gap, scrabbling with his feet to get through the hole. His body disappeared, and then a hand reappeared and gave the thumb's up.

It was strange inside the café. Huge grey ropes of cobwebs hung from the lights to the tables, and out to the chairs. The pictures on the wall were ripped and torn, and some of the furniture was broken and overturned. Daylight was fading, and the low light filled the ghostly room with an eerie glow.

It's like something out of Dickens. Great Expectations, was it? Miss Haversham? Mum liked that when it was on the telly. Now, how do I get across the main road without being seen?

Toby opened the door into a small courtyard and slipped out, staying close to the side of the building. He crept to the edge of the wall and looked left and then right. What he saw next froze his heart.

On the other side of the road was a monumental gothic-looking building, with tall spires and fancy turrets and towers. Sitting in the immense doorway was Cerberus, surrounded by his bodyguards.

17. The World Explodes

As Toby stood hidden in the shadows, he watched a parade of dogs coming and going from the college. Cerberus sat and watched with interest as each dog approached him and submissively licked its lips. Some of them rolled over in front of him, and with some he put his paw across their necks.

What are they doing in there? Starting a university?

Toby hoped the badger juice was still working, as he was only yards away from the procession of dogs. He had to get back and warn Jamie. If Jamie made too much noise clearing the rockfall, it might attract the dogs to the cellars and then they would be discovered.

He slid slowly back along the wall, his heart thumping so loud against his ribs that he felt sure the dogs must hear it. He gulped with relief once he was back inside the spooky café, and crouched down to drop himself through the hole in the floor to the tunnel below.

Without Jamie there to help, he had to leave the glass pane sitting on the café floor and hope the dogs didn't find the entrance to the tunnels.

Back in the chamber, Jamie was busy scraping frantically at the rock pile. He had cleared a good-sized hole with the help of Belle, who was using both her front paws to dig the stones away.

"You're back quick," he puffed, stopping for breath, as Toby joined him in the hectic digging.

"I've seen Cerberus; he's holding court at the college. That's why your mum can't escape that way. The place is alive with dogs. There are hundreds of them."

"What? Quick, we've got to get her out." Jamie scrabbled desperately at the mound.

"We mustn't make too much noise. The dogs will hear us," warned Toby.

The boys tore and clawed at the powdery rubble, their hands sore and bleeding. Toby's bandaged hand became even filthier with dust and grime. He tried not to think of the pain.

Must concentrate on getting Jamie's mum out of here. Then I can think about finding medicines for Sylvie.

Through the dusty air came the distinct sound of

tapping. It was getting louder and more urgent. Finally Jamie sat back and, wiping the grime from his face, said, "I can see something moving! There's something there!" He moved a large stone carefully to one side, and revealed a hand holding a large pebble. The hand was knocking the pebble against a boulder. *Tap, tap, tap!*

"Mum!" Jamie whispered hoarsely. "Mum!" He crawled forwards on his belly and grabbed the hand. They boys could hear a sob coming from the other side of the cleft in the rocks.

"Jamie? Oh, Jamie, I knew you would find me!" cried the muffled voice. "Jamie, hurry! The dogs are in the cellars; they're getting closer."

The boys redoubled their efforts and soon the hole grew bigger, and then …

"Mum!" Jamie gasped as he caught sight of his mum. She was lying, covered in dust and shale, with her legs half covered with boulders. "Mum? What happened?" He wriggled through the gap and grabbed his mum in a huge hug.

"Steady," she said, fending him off. "I'm a bit bruised. The roof collapsed and I just didn't quite make it. I'm OK, I think. Nothing feels broken. But I can't move; these boulders are pinning down my legs."

"It's OK. Everything's going to be OK now," gabbled Jamie. "I've got my friend Toby with me. He's really brave and great and … He's the one who got me and Belle here. We'd never have made it without Toby."

Under the sweat and dirt on his face, Toby felt himself going pink.

"Toby, come and meet my mum. We need to dig her out. She's stuck."

Toby crawled through to join him. Belle pushed her way past him and bounded up to Jamie's mum, licking at her face and hands.

"Hiya, Belle!" Jamie's mum greeted the dog warmly. "Have you been having an adventure?" Belle furiously wagged her tail.

Toby and Jamie gently lifted the heavy rocks from Jamie's mum's legs. She groaned and tentatively stretched them.

"How long have you been here, like this?" asked Toby, picking away at the stones.

"I don't know," she replied. "I went down to the beach café on the sixth of June to wait for you, Jamie. But when you didn't turn up, I laid a trail back here, just in case you'd got the days mixed up."

"Me? Get the days mixed up?" snorted Jamie. "It was you got the days mixed up Mum. *Today* is the sixth."

Toby decided not say anything about Jamie thinking that the day before had been the sixth. *Best to keep quiet*, he thought.

"There'd been a storm, the night before," continued Jamie's mum, "and the rain had pelted down. When I got back to the tunnels they were gushing with water from the drains. It must have loosened the rock, because as I was coming up this last bit there was a rockfall behind me, and then this one fell just as I was passing under it."

"Don't worry, Belle found a gap in the first one," Toby told her. "We'll be able to get back. Come on, we'd better move. Can you walk OK?" He offered her his hand and helped her to her feet.

"Yeah, I was really lucky. Just swallowed a lot of rock dust," she said, feeling her arms and legs. "As I thought, no breaks."

"Mum, Toby's sister is really ill. He needs to find some medicine. Can you help?"

"What kind of medicine?" she asked.

"We don't really know but antibiotics seemed to be working before we ran out. Now she's got a really high fever," replied Toby. Jamie's mum smiled.

"You're in luck, young man. I've been stockpiling stuff in the Inversneckie Café. I've found loads of medicines, and all sorts of provisions in the Offshore Survival Centre."

Toby chuckled. "That's where I was going to look for some."

"Yeah? Well, there's nothing left now. I managed to move most of it, but someone else thought of it too and the place is wrecked. Could have been the dogs, I suppose."

"Just as well we rescued Mum first then, wasn't it?" said Jamie. "You'd have got there and found nothing."

The three of them, and Belle, squeezed back through the hole in the rubble and started to make their way back through the vaulted chamber and down the tunnel. They climbed up the second pile of rocks and clambered through the gap into the tunnel that led back down towards the sea. As they went Toby recounted his visit to Marischal College, and the sight of Cerberus sitting on the steps, like a king on a throne.

"Yes, I've been keeping an eye on him," said Jamie's mum. "His power has grown enormously lately. He seems to be in control of all the dog packs in the area."

Jamie told her about Cerberus going to Collieston, and about their escape in the dinghy.

"He followed us back to Aberdeen. Why?" asked Toby.

"I don't know," replied Jamie's mum. "He seems to be keeping a watch on all human activity. Perhaps he thinks it'll lead him to food supplies. He's very clever. You'd almost think he had a plan."

"Dogs can't plan, can they?" questioned Jamie.

"These are no ordinary dogs. I'm working on a theory that …"

"Hush!" cried Toby.

A rumbling noise was rolling up from the bottom of the tunnel towards them. It was followed by a series of crashes like claps of thunder. The whole tunnel shook and a shower of shale fell on to their heads.

"What was that?" exclaimed Jamie.

"I don't know but it seems to be coming from the beach," cried Toby, shaking the dust from his hair. "We need to get out of here — now!"

The three of them stumbled and slid down the slimy passageway, trying to hold on to the cold wet walls. Jamie's mum leant on her son as she limped along, while Toby scouted ahead with Belle at his heels.

Another violent crash rent the air, and more dirt fell on their heads.

"We're getting closer to whatever's going on," said Toby worriedly, "but we don't have much choice. There's only one way out of this tunnel and that's straight into what sounds like a full-scale war!"

They crept slowly towards the ladder where they had descended into the tunnel.

"I think it's safer to follow the tunnel down to the beach where it comes out," said Jamie's mum. "I'm not sure I'll get up the ladder, anyway. I've been out of the tunnel that way before. It leads to near the golf links."

As they staggered along the last stretch of tunnel, an orangey-pink light glowed from the entrance. Suddenly the tunnel was filled with a screaming noise like something in a firework display.

"That sounded like a rocket," said Toby.

The small party reached the end of the tunnel where it spilled out on to the beach. The sea to the right was bathed in the reflected light from a blaze in the harbour, which sent flames leaping skywards and orange sparks spitting into the night.

"What's going on?" cried Jamie.

"Look!" yelled Toby. "There!" He pointed across to the mouth of the harbour where, illuminated in the flickering light, sat the sleek grey shape of a warship. "It's the frigate! It must be the *pirates* blowing up the harbour!"

As they watched, the guns bristling on the deck of the frigate fired another volley of ammunition, hitting the mangled heaps of ships in front of them. Toby, Jamie and his mum covered their ears with their hands as the blasts shook the ground.

"Why are they doing that?" screamed Jamie above the racket.

"Maybe trying to blast their way into the harbour?"

screamed Toby back. "Looks like the harbour is packed with wrecked ships."

"Or perhaps they're trying to scare anyone or anything away," said Jamie's mum. "This will send the dogs crazy; they won't hang around in Aberdeen with all this going on."

There was a lull in the bombardment and the only noise was the cracking and popping of the fire as the ships lay broken and burning.

"I need to go," said Toby determinedly. "I need to get the medicine and find some fuel. You two go for the boat. I'll meet you opposite this entrance. If I'm not back in an hour, go without me."

"No!" cried Jamie. "We wouldn't do that."

"Toby, listen," said Jamie's mum. "I hid everything in the roof space in the Inversneckie Café. You need to stand on the counter and slide off the panel in the ceiling directly above your head. It's all there."

Great! I spent hours sitting next to that counter, and all the time the medicine was above my head!

Toby nodded. Jamie's mum continued, "If for some reason you don't meet up with us, take my kayak. It's hidden behind the café, under a pile of rubbish. If we have to move we'll wait for you on the other side of the estuary. It'll be safer there. Oh, I nearly forgot — my bike's at the back of the café too. Take that; it'll be quicker than going on foot."

Toby nodded again. A bike would make all the difference, and if he did attract the attention of any dogs, he might be able to outrun them.

Toby left Jamie and his mum crouched in the entrance of the tunnel, and ran stealthily up the beach. Yellow and orange light flickered from the harbour, showing him the way across the pebbles and sand, back up to the row of cafés. He sprinted round the back of the buildings, keeping flat against the walls. The dogs may have run away from the cacophony of destruction in the harbour, but he wasn't taking any chances. Behind the café he raked through the mounds of litter. Jamie's mum had been right — the kayak and bike were still there, hidden under layers of soggy cardboard and piles of empty plastic bottles.

He had taken Jamie's torch with him and, turning it on, shone the light into the café. It was just as they had left it.

He climbed over the rubbish and into the kitchen. Hauling himself on to the counter, he stretched up and, with the tips of his fingers, pushed at one of the ceiling panels. It moved.

As Toby strained and pushed harder, the panel popped up and he managed to slide it to one side. A hole appeared over his head, and a rope dangled down from it. He gave the rope a gentle tug and heard something scraping along the roof space above. He tugged again and a large rucksack flopped over the hole. Another tug and he caught the bag as it fell to the counter.

Ripping open the cord tie on the mouth of the rucksack with trembling fingers, he shone the torch inside. It was crammed with small white boxes. He frantically grabbed one and pulled it out. Printed on the side it had a list of medical sounding names. Toby recognised one of them — penicillin! That's what he was looking for!

Toby thrust the box back into the rucksack, drew the cord shut and leapt off the counter. He dragged the rucksack straps over his shoulders and stumbled out into the night air as the sky lit up with more flashes. The bombardment had started again.

Toby picked up the bike and heaved it on to the tarmac road. He could feel the bike trembling as the vibrations of the blasts juddered through the ground. Toby flinched as the bangs and crashes thundered from the explosions.

Now where? Where am I going to get fuel from?

Toby watched the rising glow from the burning ships and knew. He *had* to go to the harbour. He remembered his dad telling him about the fuel tanks at Peterhead harbour. There would be the same here at Aberdeen. Somewhere on the quayside would be huge cylindrical tanks, hopefully with some diesel still left in.

I've no choice. I must go to the harbour! I only hope the pirates haven't blown up the tanks, along with the ships.

Toby swung his leg over the bike and set off, pedalling as fast as he could.

This has got to be the maddest thing I've done yet!

18. In the Heat of the Night

As Toby sped along the beach promenade, he realised that he'd left the empty fuel can in the dinghy. His heart sank.

Oh no. Something else to think about. Better hope there's some lying around the fuel depot.

He whizzed down the streets of the tiny fishing village of Footdee, which nestled at the edge of the harbour, his bike bumping over the cobbles. He knew the frigate must be lying at the mouth of the harbour, on the other side of the cottages. The pirates wouldn't be able to see him. Besides, they were too busy creating Armageddon.

The guns fell silent. Toby could hear shouting and screaming. Were they preparing to launch a craft and go onshore?

This is bad timing. What if they want the same thing as me?

Fuel. Maybe they're just reloading the rocket launchers? What if they fire a rocket at the fuel depot while I'm there?

Toby felt the familiar clutch of fear and panic clawing at the bottom of his stomach, drawing it into a tight ball.

As he drew closer to the granite walls of the main harbour basin, he could feel the air getting hotter and hotter. Sweat trickles prickled his eyes and his t-shirt stuck to his back. Hazy clouds of smoke floated down to the sea, filling the air with an acrid smell of burnt rubber, wood and molten metal.

Toby stood up on his pedals and scanned for the characteristic shapes of the fuel tanks in the patches of darkness ahead.

Suddenly he threw his brakes on hard and stopped. There in front of him was Aberdeen harbour. Its two main channels were crammed with the dark shapes of ships, their masts and aerials sticking up like antennae from a crazy-looking mound of insects.

Viewed through the wobbling air of the heat haze, it looked to Toby like a scene from one of those World War Two movies that his dad had liked to watch on a wet Sunday afternoon. There were ships piled on top of other ships. There were ships on fire, mere metal skeletons burning like dry sticks. There were ships sinking into the dirty black water. Some had mounted the quayside and lay tipsily on their sides, half submerged.

Ah! There they are!

Three tall towers poked their noses up from the blackness of the quayside. Toby raced towards them, feeling the scorching heat from the fires burning his cheeks.

The spiralling flames licking at the ships threw violent shadows up against the metal fences of the depot. Toby thought he saw demons and monsters lurking at every turn. He screeched to a halt in front of the fuel tanks, gravel spitting from under the bike's tyres.

Phew! Lucky!

Lying scattered around the depot were empty plastic jerrycans. Toby grabbed one and headed for the boom sticking out of one of the towers. On the end of the boom was a nozzle, like one he had seen in petrol stations. As he neared the metal tank, a wave of heat hit him. He felt like the air was being scorched from his lungs. He tore off his hoodie and, wrapping it around his face, breathed through the cloth.

It's so hot! This tank could ignite any moment!

He wrenched the nozzle from the boom with his bandaged hand.

What if they start firing again now? Don't think about it! Concentrate on the job.

He pointed the nozzle into the fuel can and squeezed it as hard as he could. At first just a dribble plopped slowly into the can.

Come ON! Please! There must be some left!

He couldn't swallow. He could feel panic tearing at his dry throat. He kept on squeezing, grimacing as the hot nozzle began to burn through the bandage. The dribble grew into a flow and within seconds a gush of diesel filled the can. Hands quivering, he screwed the cap on the can and dragged it to his bike. The heat was unbearable. He had to get out of there fast.

The bike was hot, the handlebars were hot, and the pedals were searing holes in his boots. Toby thought he was about to spontaneously combust.

Bike! Harder! Go! GO! GO!

He could smell a warm rubbery smell as the bike tyres softened in the heat. He hung on to the jerrycan with one hand and steered shakily back the way he had come — back along the quayside and towards Footdee, where he had to stop. The weight of the can was too much; he needed to swap arms. Toby turned and looked at the scene of devastation behind him. Great fountains of brilliant sparks shot into the air from one of the ships, throwing light on to the main quay. Toby caught a glimpse of a lone dog, thrown into relief, watching the harbour. It stood like a statue staring into the night.

Cerberus. What's he doing? I can't see any other dogs — have they panicked and deserted him? Why isn't he scared? I am!

Toby jumped as another rocket blasted from the

pirates' frigate. As it screeched through the air, he saw Cerberus rise on his hind legs, as if in defiance, pawing the air. Then he turned and loped away into the dark.

Where's he going? I wonder if we'll ever see him again.

Toby spun the bike round and headed for the beach, cycling as fast as the can jolting by his side would allow. The air grew cooler but was still thick with the smoky haze that billowed across the promenade. The rucksack began to slip off his shoulders and dig into the soggy t-shirt on his back. He stopped to wriggle it straight. Something darted across the road in front of him.

No! Just when I thought I was safe from the dogs!

Another shadow flitted down a side path, away from the beach. Then another, and another. There were dozens of them. The dogs were travelling fast, heads down, noses to the floor, tails tucked in between their legs. They didn't stop to look at him. They weren't interested in him at all. They were running as fast as they could out of the city. They were leaving Aberdeen.

Toby scoured the beach for any sign of Jamie and his mum. At first he could see nothing but the shadowy sands, dancing with the flickering light from the blazing harbour. But then, as he was wondering how to fit the large, lumpy rucksack and the jerrycan of fuel into the kayak, something moved near the sea's edge. He squinted into the gloom and made out two figures climbing into a boat. Belle was splashing around in waves next to them.

"WHOA! I'm here!" he shouted, not caring who heard any more. The dogs were beating a hasty retreat and the pirates were blowing up the city. "WAIT FOR ME!"

He threw the bike down and jumped up and down, waving his arms. Jamie and his mum didn't look up. They were busy packing something into the dinghy. Toby grabbed the jerrycan and ran, the rucksack bumping around on his back.

"STOP!" he yelled, struggling down the promenade steps on to the stony beach. "STOP!"

He could see Jamie's mum struggling into the boat, while Jamie pushed it away from the shore and then ran into the waves to leap on to the bow.

Toby dragged the heavy can over the rough stones and shaley sand, tears of frustration dripping down his face.

"Wait!" he cried, coming to a dead halt. He couldn't go any further. His arms were falling off and his legs had turned to jelly. He dropped to his knees on the wet sand.

"I can't go on! I can't do it!" he sobbed.

Get up, you big baby! Stop crying! What would Mum say if she could see you now? What about Sylvie? She needs that medicine right away! GET UP!

Toby hauled himself to his feet, and with his very last ounce of energy, picked up the can and the rucksack. He looked up to where he had last seen the dinghy. It was still there. Jamie had seen him and was pulling it back to the shore, helped by the incoming tide.

Toby staggered the last desperate footfalls as Jamie hung gamely on to the dinghy's tether.

"Toby! Cool! You made it! We thought you were ..."

"I didn't think I was going to make it," Toby sniffed, wading into the waves.

Jamie took the can and hoisted it on board, followed by the rucksack. He clambered over the side into the boat and then yanked Toby in beside him.

"Time to go home, hero!" Jamie called out. In the warm orange-red glow, Toby saw a huge smile crease Jamie's grubby face.

"Yeah, time to go home," agreed Toby.

The dinghy swung left and headed north.

As the tired crew made their way up the coastline, a pale pink light suffused the sea as the sun started to peek over the horizon. The journey was quiet and uneventful; the little dinghy chugged along, hugging the shore. They didn't speak; they were too exhausted for words. They stopped once to fill up the fuel tank.

Toby trusted Jamie now, so gave him the tiller, and sat with the telescope, surveying the pinkish landscape in the early dawn. As they skimmed the edge of the suburbs, from Aberdeen to Balmedie, he saw dark figures moving silently across the land. Many more dogs were running away from the city.

But they're not running in blind panic. Not like when Monty used to run away from fireworks. It looks as if they all know where they're going, perhaps staying safe until the chaos dies down. Maybe Cerberus does have a plan.

Toby's own plan was to get home as quickly as possible and, after giving Sylvie her medicine, all he wanted to do was curl up in his cosy bed and sleep for a week. How great would that be? He was tired of being brave.

The sun was fully risen when Jamie finally navigated the dinghy round the last cliff and into the bay at Collieston. Jamie's mum smiled at Toby's weary face.

"Not long before you can go to your bed," she said.

Toby smiled back, but then, as he looked over her shoulder towards the lighthouse, his smile froze.

The *Lucky Lady* had gone.

19. A New Journey

Toby leapt on to the jetty and ran up the path to the compound. The double gates swung to and fro in the breeze. There were signs of a hasty departure: empty boxes lay strewn around and a few white feathers fluttered in the corner of the yard. That was the only sign of the chickens.

He ran inside, up the stairs and through the hatch into the kitchen. Stuff lay everywhere. Things had been pulled out of cupboards then discarded on the floor. Henry's hutch on the top of the dresser had gone.

Toby frantically scrabbled through the papers and colouring books on the table, looking for a note from his dad to tell him where they'd gone. But all he could find was the picture of an orange clown on stilts he had drawn for Sylvie.

Dad! Why haven't you left me a note? For God's sake! I've rushed to get the antibiotics for Sylvie and she's not here! Where are you?

A horrible thought crossed his mind. What if something terrible had happened to Sylvie? What if his dad had lost the plot and taken off in the *Lucky Lady*? What if he was too late?

Toby ran up the stone steps to his dad's bedroom. It was in a chaotic mess, with clothes and toys littering the floor, but there was no one there.

He ran on up to the lamp room, leaping the wooden steps two at a time. The strong sunlight reflecting off the lenses made him squint and screw his eyes up. The telescope was still sitting on the tripod. He put the eyepiece to his eye, and swivelled it round 180 degrees, panning from the bay across the sea. The sea looked intensely blue in the clear, bright light. Waves foamed and broke in the mild wind. But there was no sign of the *Lucky Lady*.

Toby ran back down to the jetty where Jamie, his mum and Belle were still sitting in the cramped dinghy.

"What d'you want to do?" asked Jamie's mum. "I don't think we should stay here. It doesn't feel safe. Your dad must have left for a reason and, by the looks of it, he left in a hurry."

Toby gulped back his tears. This wasn't how it was

supposed to end. He was going to return as a conquering hero and present his dad with the medicines like a trophy from a war. Why wasn't his dad here?

"Listen," cried Jamie, "there's somebody coming!" From around the headland the heavy throb of a large boat engine could be heard, and then behind it came the familiar *chug, chug* of another, smaller engine. It was too late to try and hide anyway, so Toby stood on the jetty and watched as, coming from the next bay up, sailed an old battered minesweeper. Bouncing behind on the wash of the minesweeper was the *Lucky Lady,* and standing waving out of the wheelhouse door was his dad.

"Dad!" shouted Toby, jumping into the dinghy. "Quick, Jamie, let's get over to *Lady.*" Toby waved back, jumping up and down with excitement.

"Steady," warned Jamie. "You'll capsize us!"

"Hurry up!" yelled Toby. "Dad! I got it! I got the medicine!" But the sound of the boats' engines drowned his cries.

The minesweeper shut off its engines and came to a halt outside the bay. It was too big a boat to come in close but the *Lucky Lady* swung in towards the jetty, and sidled to a halt as the dinghy pulled alongside. Toby threw the tether to his dad, and scrambled quickly on deck.

"Toby! I thought I'd never see you again!" cried his

dad, hugging him. "I should be cross with you going off like that, you …"

"Dad! Dad! I got the medicine! I got it, Dad! And I got Jamie's mum — and she's a doctor!" squeaked Toby, as his dad's hug squeezed all the air out of him.

"You did? Wow! I can't believe it! I thought you were mad going off like that."

"How's Sylvie?" asked Toby breathlessly. "Where is she? Is she alright?"

"She's asleep in the cabin. She's not woken all day." His dad's face showed how worried he was.

"Quick," said Toby. "We must get Jamie's mum to look at her.

Jamie and his mum were clambering up on to the deck. Belle jumped up beside them, her tail wagging furiously.

"Hi," said Jamie's mum, smiling at Toby's dad. His dad smiled tiredly back.

"Quick, through here," he said, leading them all through to the cabin. "Sorry, my name's Dave Tennant. I'm Toby and Sylvie's dad," he added, holding out his hand. Toby was surprised to see his dad blushing as Jamie's mum took his hand and shook it firmly.

"Hi, I'm Katie McTavish, Jamie's mum. Thank you for taking care of Jamie and Belle. Let's see about this patient then …" She crouched down at Sylvie's bedside.

"Hello, Sylvie, sweetheart ... wakey-wakey. My name is Katie. I'm a doctor and I'm here to help." She put her hand on Sylvie's brow. Sylvie opened her eyes blearily. "We're terrified it could be ..." whispered his dad.

"Don't worry. I doubt it, Dave; it's unlikely this long after the epidemic. Everyone who survived is likely to be immune," Jamie's mum said reassuringly. "Sylvie? Can you open your mouth for me?"

Sylvie opened up and Katie took a good look inside.

"It looks like a bad case of tonsilitis to me — and the rash is a side effect of her high temperature. You wouldn't get enormous tonsils like that with red fever! The antibiotics we've brought back will take care of it, no problem."

Toby's dad lifted him off the floor with an enormous hug, tears welling in his eyes. "This is great news! Thank you!. Thank you so much."

"Thank Toby. He was the one that rescued me and Jamie and Belle. *And* got the antibiotics back to you," said Katie, patting them both on the back.

Jamie stood behind her, enthusiastically patting Belle and smiling fit to burst.

"Yes! You're right! Well done, Toby!" cried his dad, the tears of happiness streaming down his face.

Toby laughed. "Get a grip, Dad! And anyhow, where did you disappear to? You gave me a right fright!"

"We had to leave in a hurry, as you can see." said his dad. The dogs have been here for days, barking and yowling. Sylvie was having nightmares, the chickens were all over the place. It was getting impossible to stay. It was more than them being after any food we might have; it was as if they were deliberately forcing us out … and then Magnus turned up."

"Who's Magnus?" quizzed Toby.

"Him over there." His dad pointed across the bows to a distant figure who was standing on the deck of the minesweeper. "He got here just in time and scared the dogs off. I decided it was time to go. Besides, two boats travelling together are safer than one."

"Where are we travelling to?" asked Toby.

"To Orkney," said his dad. "Magnus comes from a commune that lives on the island. He's being sailing along the north-east coast looking for survivors. We're lucky he found us."

Maybe the Lucky Lady *'s not so unlucky after all. Perhaps this is the start of something new — getting away from the lighthouse with all its memories.*

Katie left to find the antibiotics that Toby had brought back in the rucksack.

"The sooner she gets some inside her, the sooner she'll feel better," she told Toby's dad.

Toby and Jamie went to help her transfer the luggage

from the dinghy to the deck of the *Lucky Lady*.

"Nice boat you've got here," Jamie's mum said to Toby's dad, as they stood on the deck watching the boys clamber into the dinghy.

"Yeah, she's a good little runner, actually," he replied. "Why don't I give you a tour once we've sorted Sylvie's medicine out?"

"Great!" replied Katie. "I love boats."

"Oh, no," groaned Toby to Jamie. "Why are parents SO embarrassing?"

Jamie giggled. "You don't think they like each other, do you?" he asked.

"Well, I think your mum will have to ditch the badger juice first!" laughed Toby.

Later that day, they all squeezed into the cabin for a hot meal of soup and crackers, followed by tinned fruit. Sylvie was sitting up on her bed looking pale but perkier. From the boxes of medicines Toby had brought back with him, Jamie's mum had sorted out a course of the antibiotics to treat Sylvie's tonsillitis. Jamie and his mum had also managed to sneak up to the café while they were waiting for Toby and bring back more food that had been hidden in the roof space.

After they had cleared away the dishes, Magnus rowed across from his boat to come and talk to them.

The adults went off to the wheelhouse to have a serious discussion about what to do next.

"That's not fair," moaned Jamie. "We should be allowed to have our say; after all, if it wasn't for you, my mum wouldn't be here."

Toby didn't mind what the adults decided. He had had enough of making decisions. It was totally overrated. He'd be quite happy for his dad to take over. He, Toby, was going to climb into his little cubbyhole in the stern, and sleep as long as he could.

When the adults trooped back into the cabin to tell them what was happening, the boys sat and listened attentively. Sylvie had gone back to sleep, with Belle cuddling up to her on the bed.

"Well, boys," said Magnus, scratching his white beard. "Looks like you'll all have to come and stay with us in Orkney, at least for the time being." Toby liked the look of Magnus. He looked like Toby imagined a sailor should, with a weather-beaten, tanned face, a shock of white hair and a beard to match. He wore a thick Guernsey jumper and a red cotton cravat round his neck.

"It's not safe around here with Cerberus and his packs of dogs. I've been analysing their behaviour and how they're developing," said Katie. "They know what they're doing — they're forcing people out and taking everything they can. And who knows what they're planning next. The pirates won't keep them away for long."

"We don't have the same problem in Orkney," said Magnus. "Smaller population meant fewer stray dogs left after the red fever."

No more dogs, no more nightmares!

"Sounds great to me!" cried Toby. "When can we go?"

"Well, I was going to take my boat down as far as Aberdeen on this trip, but from what you've told us about the pirates blowing up the place, perhaps it would be best to keep away. So, we'll set sail right away," Magnus told them

"Magnus says he's plenty of fuel, as the oil refinery at Scapa Flow has still got loads. So he's going to tow the *Lucky Lady* all the way. That will save our fuel and means that I can have a nice long nap!" Toby's dad grinned. Toby hadn't seen his dad so positive for ages.

"You can all come and stay with me on the HMS Kirkwall. Mrs McTavish can even have her own cabin," said Magnus.

"Cool," said Jamie's mum.

"What about me? Can I have a cabin?" Sylvie's croaky voice squeaked out. Everyone laughed.

"Yes," replied Magnus, "as long as you promise to keep that rabbit hutch clean!"

"You don't have a telly and a DVD of *The Little Mermaid*, do you?" Sylvie asked sleepily.

"No, I'm sorry, lass, I don't," said Magnus. Toby went and gave Sylvie a hug.

"Don't worry, Sylvie," he said. "I promise that one day you and I will watch *The Little Mermaid* again, together."

"Thanks, Tobes, I love you too," yawned Sylvie, then rolled over and went back to sleep.

The sun was dipping down behind the rolling fields beyond the cliffs, as the two boats pulled away from the north-east coast and headed out into the open seas. As Toby looked back, a solitary black dog appeared, watching them leave. Cerberus, guarding his territory. In a way, he had won: he had forced them out. But they were alive and safe, which was all that mattered. And they were on their way to a new life. Toby shuddered, breathed a sigh of relief, and looked away.

The workmanlike minesweeper dwarfed the *Lucky Lady* as she waggled behind it, like a duckling in the wake of its mother. Toby was sitting in front of the minesweeper's wheelhouse, leaning against the long shaft of a gun.

"That's a Bofor canon, is that," said his dad, sitting down to join him.

Toby looked up and smiled. "I've seen enough guns to

last me a lifetime," he said. "My ears are still ringing with all those explosions."

"That must have been scary, Toby. I wanted to say how proud I am of you, and that I'm sorry, really sorry about …"

"You don't have to say, Dad. I know," interrupted Toby.

"No, I do have to say it. I blamed you for Mum's death, and that was wrong of me. I see that now. I'm so sorry," said his dad. Toby lent over and squeezed his dad's hand.

"Dad, I understand. It was a horrible time for all of us." His dad put his arm around him and hugged him close.

"Thanks, Toby. It's time to put that behind us now, and look to the future. Thank god, Sylvie's going to be OK, and that's all down to you, Toby. We'll start a new life in Orkney."

"Just one thing, Dad. What happened to the chickens?" asked Toby. His dad smiled.

"Don't worry about them," he said. "They're all as cosy as could be in *Lady*'s engine room. I wasn't going to leave them behind for the dogs!"

"Well, I'm not offering to muck them out!" Toby said. His dad laughed and Toby laughed too.

Everything's going to be OK. Things are going to be

different. All I've got to do now is find a DVD of The Little Mermaid *for Sylvie. Oh, and find some way of playing it. After this mission, that's got to be a doddle!*

Read on for the thrilling first chapter of *Black Tide*, the sequel to *Red Fever*, where wolves, wild dogs and pirates fight to survive in this terrifying post-apocalyptic world.

1. Kidnapped

Something was wrong. In the fuggy state between slumber and waking Toby could sense something wasn't right with his world. He tried to open his eyes but sleep had a strong grip on him and he couldn't shake it loose.

Wake up! I must wake up! he told himself.

With a huge effort Toby squinted out of one eye, rubbing the other with a grimy hand. Blackness was all around him and for a moment he couldn't work out where he was. He groped to feel for the torch that was tucked in beside him and, grasping the handle, quickly wound it up. It threw a pale flickering light on the inside of the tiny cabin.

Ah, I'm in my den, thought Toby.

For a moment he felt reassured. This was his safe

place where he came to hide from the madness outside that was now his life. But as he lay curled up on the old mattress that took up most of the space, Toby felt a growing unease. There was something *so* strange about the way the boat was pitching and rolling sideways. Toby had hated sailing but since the red fever had changed everything in the past three years, he had had to learn the ways of the sea. He had had no choice; it was that or not survive.

A terrible sense of dread crept over him and, fighting his terror, he pulled on his damp clothes, keeping an ear open for any noise. There was no sound of the *Lucky Lady's* engine, there was no sound of his dad or his little sister Sylvie. There was no sound of anything except the *whack, whack, whack* of the waves hitting the side of the boat as it was tossed and thrown about.

What's going on? Why aren't we moving? The boat feels like it's drifting. What's Dad doing?

Toby felt sick as he crawled to the hatch door and flipped it open, shading his eyes to the brightness of the morning light. Something felt wrong, terribly wrong. As he swung round to face the *Lucky Lady's* cabin Toby saw exactly what it was. There standing on the deck were two huge men dressed in black, their backs towards him. Toby froze, the cold hand of fear closing over his heart.

"Hey! You two! Come in here and help me tie the

prisoners up!" shouted a gruff voice from the cabin.

"Yep Captain!" one of the men shouted back. The two men stooped and disappeared through the low wooden door of the boat's cabin.

Prisoners? thought Toby. *Whoever is in the cabin must be talking about Dad and Sylvie. We must have been boarded by pirates!*

Toby now saw the grey outline of a large inflatable boat moored alongside the *Lucky Lady*. He pulled himself up onto the deck and, grasping the rail, made his way unsteadily towards the cabin as the boat bucked and shifted under his feet.

What are they doing with Dad and Sylvie? What do they want with them? Surely they just want to steal our food and fuel? These can't be ordinary pirates.

Toby felt a hot anger rising in his chest as he thought of the dirty rough men pulling his little sister Sylvie around. She was only six years old and though she could be very annoying at times, Toby was always fiercely protective of her. After all, she had no mum to look after her now.

What am I going to do? There are at least three of them and they are enormous and probably have weapons! How am I going to fight them off?

Toby slunk down and crawled nearer to the cabin door. He could hear raised voices from within.

"Take your filthy hands off us!" an angry voice rang out. It was his dad. "Why are you doing this? What do you want with us? Just take our food and fuel!"

Toby heard a loud coarse laugh and then someone said, "We don't want your meagre offerings! It's *you* we want!"

There was a scream from Sylvie as sounds of a scuffle came from the open door. Toby's blood started to boil. How dare these evil men board their boat and assault his family. He had to do something and he had to do it now.

He glanced round, searching for something he could use to defend himself and spied a large wooden pole with a hook on the end that they used to pull the boat to moorings. Toby picked it up and without thinking flung himself through the cabin door.

What he saw inside made him cry out in fear and dismay; his dad and Sylvie were cowering in terror on one of the bunk beds, their hands tied in front of them. Standing over them were four men, filling the tiny cabin with their bulky frames, all of them wielding guns. The men turned and stared in shock at the young boy waving a pole at them. Toby didn't hesitate.

"Take that!" he screamed as he lunged at the one nearest him, striking out with the hook and cracking the man violently across the top of his skull. The man crumpled slowly to the floor with a quiet moan, but before Toby could raise his pole for another attack on the next man, someone cannoned into him and smacked him heavily to the hard floor of the cabin.

The last thing that Toby was aware of was the concerned voice of his dad ringing in his ears: "Toby? Toby? What have you done to him?"

It was some time later when Toby started to come to. His head throbbed, and through the misty fog of pain he was aware of someone standing over him.

The man called out, "Is there any point in taking this one? He looks at death's door. Must have hit his head hard. Does the General want damaged goods?"

"Aye! Chuck him into the inflatable along with the others. If he looks a goner we'll throw him overboard," called back another.

Toby felt someone lift him clumsily, carry him out of the cabin into the cold air and then throw him into empty space. He gasped as he felt himself fly through the air and then hit the wooden planking at the bottom of the inflatable. As he lay, unable to open his eyes, he heard his dad murmuring to Sylvie nearby. He could smell the metallic tang of blood somewhere nearby, and tried to put his hands to his head, which felt wet and sticky, but his hands were tied together. Someone's boot nudged him sharply in the ribs.

"Leave my brother alone!" he heard Sylvie squeal.

"Tell your kid to shut up or else she'll end up like her big brother," a voice commanded.

"Don't you touch a hair on her head!" shouted back his dad. This was followed by bursts of laughter from the four men.

"Like you can do anything about it, eh?" said the same man. Toby could hear a tone of authority in his voice and wondered if he was the Captain the men referred to. "Now you tell your kids to behave," the man continued, "and we'll all get along just fine. It's not in our interest to knock you about – we want you to arrive in one piece otherwise you'll not be much use to us."

"Aye," cried out another voice, "otherwise it'll be us that'll get it in the neck from the General!"

"Shut up Calvert! Else I'll have to shut you up too!" barked the Captain.

Toby lapsed in and out of the darkness of unconsciousness as the inflatable's outboard motor roared into life and the boat took off, bouncing over the waves. He could feel his dad's hand grasping roughly onto his, and as he peered painfully into the light he saw his dad and Sylvie crouching in the bottom of the boat next to him.

Where are they taking us? Toby thought, gritting his teeth as the boat hurtled along, banging violently against the waves and sending spasms of pain ripping through his body.

"You'll like it at Fort George," shouted the Captain, as if reading Toby's thoughts. "We've collected quite a number of folks just like you – loners struggling to survive in this mad world. You'll thank us for rescuing you from your pitiful life. At least you'll have company!"

"What do you want with us?" his dad shouted back over the drone of the engine.

The men laughed again, and one replied, "That'll be a surprise for you to look forward to!"